ROYALLY CLAIMED

A SPICY SPACE OMEGAVERSE ROMANCE

JUPITER BELLE

Copyright © 2022 by Jupiter Belle

All rights reserved.

No part of this book may be reproduced in any form or by any electronic or mechanical means, including information storage and retrieval systems, without written permission from the author, except for the use of brief quotations in a book review.

This is for me. And for Bree on Mondays.

CHAPTER 1

IT WAS COLD OUT. STUPID, UNGODLY, PAINFULLY cold. The kind of cold that slices through your clothing no matter how many outerwear layers and wool socks you are wearing. I wrap my arms around myself and duck my head, chin tucked to my chest. As it was, I wasn't really wearing much against the winter storm I currently found myself in. What the hell had I been thinking, leaving my house with nothing but a goddamn hoodie that I had swiped from the back of the couch?

Oh right. I knew exactly what I'd been thinking when I'd stormed out of the party I'd been at.

"Fuck, Ben," I snarl, teeth gritted against the blast of cold air that hit me in the face. If anyone saw me they would be within their rights to tell me my face was going to "get stuck like that" if I didn't stop. Snow and wind were pelting me, making me drop my snarl, biting my bottom lip so hard I could taste blood. "That fucking asshole!" I stomp my foot for emphasis and nearly eat shit on the icy sidewalk. I growl and keep moving forward. I didn't know where the hell I was going, but I did know it wasn't home. Home was where Ben was with all of his stupid, fancy, *pretty* friends.

His pretty friends he was totally banging behind my back.

Ben was, no, he *had* been, my boyfriend. And the problem that had sent me straight out into the night was that Ben was *definitely* fucking the hot blonde in his PhD program. I'd caught them red-handed, pants down and dick out, in his bedroom.

I should have seen it coming by the longer "research hours" he'd been pulling, or the long lunches he seemed to have made a habit of lately. Not to mention the flirty glances that had started the second the woman had stepped foot in our house, and the little ways she'd been touching him all night. Yes, my red flag radar had gone off when I'd seen them together, heads bent close and murmuring as they poured wine together and laughed. But who was I to be suspicious of a friendship? I mean, there had been the looks his cohort had sent my way throughout the evening. I hadn't understood them then, but now I did.

Pity.

They had felt sorry for me in my own damn home. I mean, counting what had happened that night under my roof, I guess a group of smartypants strangers feeling sorry for me wasn't the worst of it.

I'd been looking for him, wanting to ask him when he wanted me to serve the Hors d'oeuvres that I'd made for the gathering. It was supposed to be casual, trendy, intimate...cozy. Whatever the hell Home and Garden buzzword Ben came up with to describe the gathering we'd been hosting for the first years in his Psych program. He was nearly at the end of it all, and we'd been together for the whole thing. Five long years with another left. Five years of me paying most of the bills. Five years of me moving us from our small apartment right off campus to the pretty little historic bungalow we were currently sharing. I paid the lion's share of the bills, covered the grocery shopping, furnished the house and was the one that paid his car, seeing as Ben was a perpetual student.

There was no shame in being a student. I knew plenty of graduate students that made a decent living, but it was because they hustled. Ben expected everything to be handed to him just because he existed. I hadn't really thought much about it. I paid for things because I had more. It had always been that way. So I think it just seemed normal to me, given the dynamic of our relationship. We were planning on getting married anyways, and I was doing just fine at my job. I worked at an investment firm. I had a head for numbers, I liked the way neat accounts made me feel, and I was damn good at following my instincts when it came to managing portfolios.

Too bad my instincts were shit when it came to being cheated on.

AND. IN. MY. HOUSE.

"This is what you get for dating pretty boys," I tell myself, blinking hard against the snow that's now coming sideways at me in the wind. I hadn't thought the weather was that bad, not when I first sprinted out of the house. It had only been lightly snowing then, a really pretty scene on the picturesque street we lived on. It was a pretty street lined with even prettier houses, and inside one of them was a pretty boy that had nailed his pretty classmate right under my damn nose.

The whole thing was ugly to me. Where was I even going? Everything looked the damn same.

Snow was falling by the bucketful around me, making it hard to see anything more than a foot or so ahead. I squinted. The streetlights overhead didn't illuminate much, just sort of broke up the gloom I was in with a patch of barely-there light. I blink and realize there are tiny icicles clinging to my lashes. When I raise my hand to rub at my eyes, I realize I'm crying.

Just because Ben was a cheater and an overall freeloader didn't mean I hadn't loved him. God, I hope I didn't still love him after this.

What the hell was I going to do?

I whimper but try to swallow the sound. It's no use, and a sob escapes my lips. Then I'm crying so hard my snot is freezing to my fucking face. "Fuck." I wipe at my nose with the cuff of my 'borrowed' hoodie and wince. I am definitely going to have to wash this before I give it back. You can't just steal a hoodie and return it full of boogers. You just don't. I stop under the light, and look down at my feet. I squeeze my eyes shut with a ragged shudder. The cold turns my breath into painful crystals the second it hits my throat. I welcome the burn, because I can think about that and not what just happened to me. But even then, with my fingers and toes going numb, the thin hoodie covered in snot, it's no use. The tears are here to stay, and that sucks.

If I had it my way I wouldn't shed a single tear for Ben Wright.

I swipe at my eyes and blow my nose again in the sleeve of the poor mystery guy's hoodie. At least I think it's a man's hoodie. It has to be, since it's so long it hits my knees and I'm not short by any stretch of the imagination. I'm 5'10, easily over 6 feet with my heels on. Ben hated it when I wore heels. I mean, I didn't really like wearing them, but I was going to wear heels every damn day so long as I knew it'd piss his cheating ass off.

I lift my head, eyes narrowing as the anger in my chest flares brightly, keeping me somewhat warm enough to keep stalking forward in the snow.

Men. Screw men. Screw all men.

Even the man whose hoodie I was snotting up. Screw him too.

I shiver and wrap my snotty sleeves around myself before I start off again. My feet are moving as fast they can in the flats I'm wearing. I hate these damn shoes. Velvet ballet flats that Ben thought looked "cute and feminine," which for some reason had become really important to the man I thought I knew. I was a tomboy. I was always more comfortable in a pair of Docs or sneakers than anything else. I wore flats for work, or a low heel to look semi-professional, but the great thing about my job was I was so good at it no one cared what I looked like so long as I was passable. I wasn't as trendy as the blonde bombshell my man had chosen over me tonight, but that was fine.

It was. It really was.

I was focused on work. Driven to reach the next level. It was an addiction, and that was fine.

My steps slow and a whisper of *why* this happened comes to me. Not why Ben cheated, but what I hadn't noticed until it was literally smacking me in the face. Ben cheated because that was who he was as a person. That was his fucking shit to unpack and had zero to do with me as a person, but still…

How had I not noticed?

That was simple. I hadn't noticed because I was lowkey more into work than my long-term boyfriend. So long as things were good at the office, I had been happy as a clam.

Work meant more to me than Ben. At work I was challenged, respected. At work I had goals and a sense of accomplishment. With Ben? I was nitpicked and sighed at for choosing to wear the same thing every date night. Who cared what I wore if I liked it? Why was he so concerned about me being seen in the same little red dress and kitten heels I loved? None of that was supposed to matter when you were in love with someone. Their clothing or shoe choices were secondary to the fact that you got to be around them, right?

I swallow hard.

"Right," I mutter to myself. It has to be true. It just has to.

I stomp harder and faster up the sidewalk. I hadn't known where I was going a second ago, but now? Now, I know. I am going home, because I pay the bills in that damn house and the lease is in my name.

So why was I out in the snow like a lost member of a settler expedition?

If anyone was going to freeze their ass off in a white-out it was Ben, not me. I try to stay upright, keeping my spine strong and all that, but it's next to impossible given the snowstorm that's hitting me square in the face.

It was fine, I hadn't gone far. I just had to power stomp a few more minutes and I'd be right back in front of my house. I swipe at my cheeks, tears sticking and turning icy on my cheeks as I do. I want to stop crying before I reach the house, though. But I can blame it on the snow or wind getting in my eyes while I Boss Babe up long enough to kick Ben's cheating ass out in the snow. I pass beneath a dim streetlight, the night eating the light before it has much of a chance to do much, and I squint.

Up ahead I see my house through the sleeting snow. I march faster now, teeth chattering and stupid velvet ballet flats slipping, pinching my frozen feet as I go. I suck in a painful breath and push myself faster towards the familiar walkway. The front door is open, only the storm door closed, showing me the brightly illuminated renaissance painting that currently is my living room.

Most of Ben's cohort is squeezed in the front room, some are spilling out into the hallway in front of the door. One of them is the blonde I caught him with. I think her name is Jenny? Megan? I'm not sure, really. Ben has his arm wrapped around her and she's crying into his side, our bedroom door open behind them.

Everyone at the party knows what I caught them doing. There's no way they don't. My pace speeds up and I feel a surge of vengeance in my heart at seeing the woman cry while Ben looks contrite and remorseful. He should be those things at the very least. The two of them. Everyone should give them shit. I hope that's why she's crying, but then I realize it's not when Ben turns her to him and kisses her in full view of everyone at the party.

I skid to a halt, ballet flats slipping and sliding out from under me at my sudden stop as I fall backwards. I'm going to hit ass first on the pavement and end up with a wet ass for all my damn righteous storming about. The people inside my house clap. They are happy about the changing of the guard. Old girlfriend out, new one in. Easy peasy.

"What the fuck, you *asshole*?!" I howl, but my scream is mostly lost in the wind. I think I see Ben turn his head to me, but everything is dark. Darker and harder to see than it was a second ago, and I'm still falling. I pinwheel my hands, trying to catch onto something, but there's nothing because I'm outside in front of my house screaming like a crazy person.

Why the hell haven't I hit my ass on the ground yet? I swipe my arm and it rushes through the air, cutting through the snow like everything is in slow-mo. I move my feet and it's then I realize, I'm not falling.

I'm floating.

Oh fuck.

CHAPTER 2

When I finally hit the ground it was with as much grace as you would expect a woman going down ass first to display. I land with a thud and a yelp, arms and legs shooting out as I hit the ground.

I groan, fall back, and wince. "This is bad," I say to no one. Except, there isn't 'no one' in the room. There are many *someones* in the room I just suddenly fell ass first into. I hear them before I see them.

There are clicks as they speak, but it's mostly guttural consonants.

Click, click, click bphm. Click!

I open my eyes when I realize it's speech, and not the result of a concussion induced hallucination. "Who are you?" I ask. "Where am I?"

A hand lands on my arm. It's a sticky damp hand, and I cringe trying to scuttle away from it but it's as strong as it is damp, and I'm yanked right back into the center of the room. My eyes widen when I look at the hand. Really, truly, look at it.

It's a green webbed hand that makes me think of the amphibian and reptile exhibit at the metro zoo I went to as a kid. I don't breathe as I look right up the arm and see that it's all green and slightly slimy. I hear more...whatever the *hell* this thing is. It highly resembles a frog? A salamander maybe? Well, except for its beak, which looks like a snapping turtle. It's big, especially for a frog-salamandar-snapping turtle mix.

"What are you?" I ask the sort of frog man.

He clicks at me and a second webbed hand lands on my shoulder. There's another creature at my side, because of course there is. I see two more in the corner of the room, fussing over a tray. I swallow hard and try not to think about what might be on that metal tray, one that looks way too much like the trays I've seen at the dentist office.

I shake my head when they try to yank me up to stand. "I must have hit my head," I try to reason.

They ignore me and drag me forward to stand by

the other two creatures by the tray. One of them turns and I see an array of gleaming instruments. I feel like I'm going to puke when one of them raises what looks like a massive dart gun, except that this is silver and shiny and has a big glass tube attached to the side of it. I gulp when I see something moving in the glass tube. There's something inside of it that's moving, or a lot of little *somethings* that are crawling up the glass, falling off and back into the squirming mass. Whatever it is that they're going to put in me is definitely *alive*.

I dig my heels in. "No way. I'm out of here," I say and try to run, but the froggy men are strong.

Really strong.

When I can't break loose from them I switch tactics. "You want money?" I ask frantically. I look at them and jerk my chin in the direction of the door I can see behind me. "I can get you money. I swear, I can. Whatever you want, how much do you need? Just-" I break off and kick a leg at the froggy man approaching me with the syringe gun in hand, "keep that shit away from me!"

There is a series of sounds and clicks between them and the one that first grabbed me draws himself up to his full height. He's much taller than me. "You don't want money? Okay, that's fine, I get it. Capitalism, *blehhh*," I say and make a face. "What *do* you want?"

The syringe gun and all it's wiggling glory gets closer, and I can see that it is 10000% totally full of living things. Things they are going to put into me. I have to do something, so I kick again and the leader grabs my flailing legs. One of my ballet flats goes flying over their head and crashes into the metal tray.

Click, click, gnthr.

Nope, they did not like that.

"I have to be dreaming. I hit my head," I hiss, about to go hysterical. "That has to be it. I hit my head. I'm laying in the snow bleeding out while my cheating boyfriend parties. The cold is making me delirious."

I struggle harder, but it's not easy given that I'm being held up by four of the froggy men, and apparently none of them have been skipping the gym. I thrash, body wiggling like a fish caught on a line, which just annoys them.

I mean, I get it. If I was trying to do my job and some lunatic was thrashing and screaming I'd be annoyed too.

Click, cliccccccck! Click, cliccccccck!

"Shit!" I scream. I hear a whirr come from the syringe gun and now it's just over my neck. I turn my head to the side, trying to roll away, but there's nowhere to go. Not with the four of them holding me like they are.

There's a click and a slide and then a shooting pain in the side of my neck, just under my ear. I gasp as the sharp pain of the *living organisms* being injected into my body hits me like a bat upside the head. A wave of nausea hits my stomach and I choke, bile rising up in my throat. "*Oh god,*" I rasp. I'm going to be sick. My insides feel like they're on fire. Like my body is expanding and shrinking all at the same time. There's a roar in my ears, a ringing that blocks out the sounds and voice around me. The froggy men have the sense to drop me, and I throw up the second my hands and knees hit the floor.

At least I didn't get it on me. My body heaves, and I puke harder, my world is dizzy and loopy. Whatever they put in me is definitely messing with my equilibrium. I fall back on my hands and suck in a ragged breath, the sour taste of my sick still in my mouth.

"When am I going to wake up?" I whisper. I don't expect anyone to answer, but four voices respond to me.

"You're property of the Magi now!"

"Human cows are *disgusting*."

"She's dumber than the last four."

"You are awake. No sleeping."

I gasp, bolting to sit upright and stare at the froggy men. "I can understand you now. Why can I understand you now?" I ask.

"Chip implant," one of them says, tapping where I guess his ears are. His skin is smooth and shiny, head round where you might think ears would be. "Plus a little something extra." My stomach turns and flips at that. What the fuck does he mean 'something extra'? I just saw real living things crawling in that tube. I don't want something extra. I don't want anything from them.

"All two thousand languages of the system are in your brain now," another says and with a snort. "Not that it'll help you."

"What? What do you mean?" I ask.

They don't answer me this time. The leader nods at the other two. "Get her up. She needs to get hosed down before the auction. She stinks."

I'm yanked up by the froggy men and half dragged out of the room. I blink, but stay quiet, because I don't know what to say. I think I'm going into shock, really. The pain from the implant is fading, but I'm reeling. I don't even know what I would say beyond what I already have. I can't get away from them.

I'm somewhere with *two thousand* languages that I can now somehow understand. I've never had an ear for languages. I can only half understand Spanish, and maybe a little French. But that was...before.

That was on Earth.

I swallow hard when a window comes into view. There's no storm there. Just inky blackness, but it isn't because it's nighttime. It's because we're in space. I can see stars dotting the black far away, but not so far away that I don't know what the hell I'm looking at. I see a small gathering of ships nearby and what looks like a giant docking station, or at least as close to the ones I saw in Sci-Fi movies.

Wherever I am now, it's not earth. It's space.

Am I even in the same solar system? I swallow hard, craning my neck to take in the space scene in front of me, but then realize it's stupid. Would I even know what to look for in space? It's not like there are signs that say Jupiter this way, or Mars back that way.

It's just...space.

Plus there's the fact that I'm being dragged down a hall by frog hybrids. This is so not my solar system.

"Where am I?" I moan. My stomach still feels unsettled, like it's full of a thousand butterflies and each and every one of them is beating their wings. It's like the thrill you get on the climb of a rollercoaster, but my feet are on solid ground (*sort of*) if you count a spaceship solid ground. Holy shit. *How am I on a spaceship?!*

"Seventh district," the one on my left grunts in answer to my question.

I blink at him, confused at his answer, because I'd already forgotten I'd even asked the question. What is going on with me? I'm all over the place. Whatever they shot me up with has to be responsible for this. I'm level-headed, sharp, quick on figuring out things, but now I can't even remember a question seconds after I've asked it. I feel scrambled. I'm sweating now and my temperature feels higher than normal. How long am I going to be like this? Yeah, it has to be the creepy crawly things they injected in me. I don't care if they said it was just a language chip.

It's either the chip, or I'm in shock.

"Don't talk to the cow," the one on my right snaps. They give me a shake and I fall silent, but I don't miss the look the one that spoke gives me. It looks pitying. I bit my lip, the cut from earlier opening up again. That's the second time in one night I've been looked at with pity. It doesn't matter that the first time it was from Ben's cohort, or that now it's from pretty much a bipedal kidnapping frog.

The looks are the same.

I grit my teeth, hating the shame that washes over me at the look, and stare ahead. The hallway floor is cold against my bare feet, but I limp along all the same, one shoe on, the other one left in the room I'd been in. It's only another minute before I'm sort of tossed in a room, this one is smaller than the last. I see a shower in one corner. My captors drag me in and shove me in the direction of the shower.

"Get in."

I wrap my arms around myself and think about arguing, but I don't. I just do what they say and get in the shower fully clothed. I wonder if they'll bark at me to get undressed, but a second later one of them hits a button to the left of them. A glass wall slides down in front of me, closing me off from them in the corner, and I'm blasted with freezing water from all ends.

I scream at the shock and throw up my hands, shielding my face from the icy water.

"*Drek*, Amon! Turn it off!" One of them yells at the other, and from the pissed look I know it's the one that pitied me. He hits the button while the other howls with laughter.

"Stop going soft, Nill. They're just animals," the other one says, tapping another button. I'm suddenly in a vortex of air. It's harsh on my sensitive skin, but thankfully it's warm. I'm dryer than I should be after thirty seconds, and the asshole who blasted me with water sighs and waves a webbed hand at me. *"Drek it.* She'll do. It's not like they'll care what she looks like. They're buying her to rut."

My stomach roils and I feel faint. I put a hand out against the wall and suck in a deep breath. I might not know what *Drek* means, or where the hell I am in the universe, but I do know that word.

Rut.

This is so bad.

"Let me go," I try, when the glass slides up and they start to move towards me again. "Please, look, you don't want me for whatever is going on. I won't say a word about any of this. I promise."

"Shut your mouth, cow," the jackass frog snaps as he grabs my arm.

The other one is quiet. There won't be any help from him on this, but it doesn't stop me from trying. "Please, help me. This is wrong. You know it is!"

I get a sharp smack to the back of my head.

"Keep quiet or you won't make it to auction," the jackass frog threatens. I go silent then. Being sold to people who want to rut you? That's bad news. But from the way he's talking, I know not making it to auction is even worse.

What the hell could be worse than being sold by aliens?

I bite my lip and keep walking, because there's nothing else I can do but that. We go through another door and, before I can get my bearings, a pair of cuffs are slapped onto my wrists. "Stay here," Jackass frog snarls, giving me a shove.

The other lingers for a minute. He shifts from foot to foot for a second but when I look up to meet his eyes, he's gone. The door slides shut behind him in a *whoosh*. I let out a shaky breath and look down at my wrists. They have shiny metallic cuffs on them, manacles really. I shake my hands, testing out the cuffs but they don't budge.

"Think, *think*," I tell myself. I turn, look around the room, and freeze. I'm not alone. There's women all over this place. "H-hello?" I call out softly. My voice shakes and I bite my bottom lip again. I hate how worried I sound, but what's a gal gonna do when she's stranded in space with an auction about to go down?

"Over here," a woman calls out to me. She's petite, red hair cropped short to her head. She waves me over. "Keep it down. You don't want them to come back here."

"What happens if they do?" I ask her.

She shudders and drops down, sitting back on her heels as she wraps her arms around her knees. "They shoot you full of stuff."

"What stuff?" I drop down beside her.

She gives a shake of her head and presses her chin to her knees. "I don't know."

"Does it move?" I ask.

She looks at me then but doesn't answer. I hear a woman arguing with someone. I look toward the noise and see there's a curtain of sorts. I frown and nod at the curtain where the woman arguing has turned into flat out yelling.

"What's going on over there?"

"The auction," the redhead tells me, a slight twang in her voice. She bites her bottom lip and then says, "I'm Rose."

"Darcy," I tell her.

"Pleased to meet ya."

"Likewise."

A woman crying softly in the corner has me feeling sick. There are five more women, all huddled like Rose and I am. This somehow feels worse than when it was just me heading up to the auction block. I have to do something.

I lift my cuffed hands. "Any idea how these work?"

She shakes her head. "Nope," she says.

I raise an eyebrow and nod down at her hands. "How come you're not cuffed?"

"I'm not a threat," she tells me, and I see her lips curve up in a smile. It's slight, but it's still there. "None of us are but you and Sally."

"That's because I punched one," A brunette with long curly hair says. She's small, elfin almost, but there's a fire in her that I like. "I socked him good. Stupid frog." She rolls her shoulders and raises her hands, flipping the bird to the curtains.

"I like you," I say.

Her lips press into a thin line, but she doesn't say anything. Instead she opts to turn her back on me and lean against a couple of crates. I shrug. She's prickly, I get it. We all got abducted by aliens and are waiting backstage at the universe's weirdest talent show. Or that's what this whole auction thing seems like when I hear a round of applause erupt from the other side of the curtains. I hold my breath, waiting to see if the woman will be led back where we are, but there's no one. Instead a voice starts to speak over a sound system, but I don't know what they are saying because the words are muffled and low.

"What happened to her?" I ask Rose.

"She got sold," Rose replies and shakes her head. "They never come back."

"How long have you been there?"

"Three weeks," she says quietly. "At least, I think so. I wouldn't really know if it wasn't for Nill."

Nill...Nill...Nill...

That seems familiar. Why do I know that name? "Uhh...and that is?"

"The nice one," Rose says. "Of the frogs."

Right. The one that looked at me with pity. "Yeah, he's all right," I settle on.

"He's still helping them sell us," Sally spits out from where she's still turned around.

Rose nods. "Yeah, there's that."

"Don't worry," I say, surprising myself. I sound confident even though I still feel sick. My temperature hasn't gone down. If anything, it's higher now. I'm sweating, but I chalk it up to the situation more than anything. My body has to be in fight or flight mode.

"I have a plan."

That gets Sally's attention. She turns around, and so does every other woman in the place.

Oops. Why did I say I had a plan? I don't even know what solar system I'm in! How the hell am I going to come up with a plan to save us? A woman already got sold off since I've been here. Just because Rose has been here for a hot minute doesn't necessarily mean I have time on my side. I look down at my feet, but my eyes land on my wrists. The shiny cuffs I wear catch my attention.

"I'm not a threat. None of us are, but you and Sally."

I smile. I'm a threat. These alien frogs know I'm one. And while it's not a huge win, it's enough to make me nod and look up at the roomful of expectant women. I'm going to prove those damn frogs right.

I *am* a threat.

CHAPTER 3

"This is never going to fucking work," Sally mutters. She's crouched beside me and I shift to the side, trying to peek around the curtains. It's no use from where we are. We're too low to see anything beyond the stairs that go up to the platform where this whole nightmare auction is happening.

"It's not like they'll care what she looks like. They're buying her to rut."

My stomach goes sour and I have to suck in a deep breath through my nose. I count to ten and force away the anxiety attack that's about to hit me square over the head. I have to be running on adrenaline. There's no other explanation for how calm I'm being. There are aliens. There are aliens that are going to buy me. There are aliens that are going to buy me to *rut*.

I wish my life was simple. Right about now I'd take Ben cheating on me any day of the week, but these are my problems. My entire world view is changed, and I'm in space trying to get the courage up to attack my frog guards.

"Oh, ye of little faith," I say, giving her a wink. "It's going to be fine. I promise." I'm totally lying through my teeth. She's right. There are definitely a million little reasons this won't work. The 'this' is us managing to knock a few frogs out. There are only the ones I've seen, so that's five in total for the ship that Rose says is a sort of pit stop on the way to the bigger ship I saw or onto whatever other star system the buyer might have in mind.

Star system.

Yup. We aren't talking about a solar system that I might know of in the singular *one,* but star systems as in there are hundreds of them out there. I don't know how she knows all of this, but I get the feeling Rose listens a lot when people don't think she is.

After we knock the frogs out we're going to make a break for the control room which Sally is pretty sure she knows the way to. She's also confident she can fly this damn thing. How does she know that?

No clue. I can barely drive manual transmission without burning out the clutch, but I like a confident woman, so I nod along with her.

"When they come back here, you know what to do," I say, leaning forward on my hands and knees to try and track the guard that's walking around. He's pacing, if I have eyes on him and the announcer is doing their whole auction schtick then I know where two of them are.

That just leaves three unaccounted for. There are eight of us and five of them. We can take them if we focus. God, I hope we can take them. I creep closer and freeze when I see the guard turn and begin to head our way.

"Bring the next one up!"

This time the announcer's voice is clear and strong. Okay, showtime.

I motion for Sally to take her spot. She's got restraints on like me, but I know she's ready to put the hurt on our captors, same as me. The other women hesitate and for one wild moment I think they aren't going to follow through on our insane plan, but Rose stamps her foot at them.

"You want to get *sold*?" she asks, already hot footing it to her spot by the door. "*Move it!*"

The women scramble to fall into position, trying

to appear nonchalant while also being within striking distance of a guard. Rose and Jasmine have the door. Sally is with me taking out the first guard, giving us double the opportunity to fight back. The other four are lounging in the middle ready to provide reinforcements to whichever side needs it. I suck in a breath and cross my arms, making a show of examining the ceiling, when the guard makes his way into the room.

"You," he says, and points a finger.

I blink because the jerk has his webbed finger pointing directly at me. Of course. *Of course* it's me. I nod, fighting down the wave of fear that blooms in my belly at the thought of taking the stage and putting our plan into action. If we don't succeed, I don't know what will happen to us. Will they sell us? Will they decide to toss us right out of the ship because we're more trouble than we're worth?

I have no idea, so I do the only thing I can and take a step forward, giving him a shaky smile.

"Lucky girl," I murmur.

He snorts and gives me an impatient wave of his hand. "Move it. We have to get through selling all of you tonight."

All of us? I glance over my shoulder at the other women when I hear the collective intake of breath.

They're scared too. That's enough to make me not feel alone, it's also enough to give me the resolve to do the thing that needs doing.

It's time to beat frog man ass.

"Move it," he orders again.

I hold up my hands and give him a smile that's all teeth. "Coming, coming."

He has a stick in his hand and I wonder if it's a weapon. He moves, turning the bottom of it, and it lights up. Yup, definitely a weapon with the way he's moving towards me now. I nod at Sally to do her thing, but she doesn't move. I bite my lip and clear my throat, but it's clear she's frozen with fear. *Fuck.* I hadn't thought that would happen. The frog guard waves the glowing stick at me. The threat is clear. Move it or you're gonna take a lighting bolt.

I move towards him.

"Easy, big guy," I say. Sally drops her eyes and I hear Rose whimper beside the door, but it's no use. The plan is shot. We are going to have to see what happens on the fly. Maybe I'll have another chance when I move onto the next section of whatever is about to happen to me. I cross my fingers, but dread is coiling tight around me.

I follow the guard out and I blink at the harsh bright lights overhead and raise my hands to shield my face. I can't see anything, it's all so bright. I swallow hard and hesitate, the guard shoving me forward until I'm standing in the middle of the stage.

"And now here we have Lot C," the announcer says. I jump, looking for the speaker and see him standing off the side. He's looking at a glass tablet. It's lit up, and when he swipes his hand across it I see specs for me flash up in front of the stage.

Darcy Luthor.
Age 28.
Origin: Earth.
Creation: Human
Designation: Omega
Status: Fertile. Start of Estrus Cycle.

I raise an eyebrow. What the fuck is an *omega*? And what the fuck do they mean fertile? Fertile for what? Es-what? What cycle?

"And where shall we start the bidding for this fine specimen of fertility and submission?" The announcer asks with a wave of his hand. "She's the only Omega on the docket for tonight, which makes this a rare find indeed. And not only that, but this one is ripe for the picking."

"Where did you get an Omega?" A muffled voice

asks from the dark. It's raspy, dark and makes me think of the grimy soot that gets stuck to your hands when you're camping and trying to put out your fire. I rub my hands against my jeans and shift. Sweat is clinging to my back and my hair feels limp and plastered to the side of my neck despite my "shower" earlier. I'm shaking. My stomach clenches and I wince at the sudden sharp cramp before I wobble and barely keep my feet under me.

"Oh, this one was specially picked. We tracked her for months to ensure the necessary genetic markers for Omega presentation."

"Humans don't present as Omegas. Everyone knows that," the raspy voice shoots back. It sounds farther away now, but I don't hear movement. Are they out there walking around? I strain my ears trying to hear a footstep, but I can't. What I can hear is the murmur of agreement, but I'm too focused on the fact that I was followed for months by these aliens to register it.

Oh. My. God.

I was getting stalked by the frogmen for months and didn't know? First Ben, and now this? Just how wrapped up in my work was I that I didn't see this coming? I start to shake, but I refuse to let them see just how much this is messing with me. I squeeze my hands together and lift my chin. I'm going to have to face this head on, because there was never an escape for me in this. It was planned. Knowing that makes me want to throw up and hide. My ears are ringing, I'm practically panting now. There's no faking even breaths, not anymore. My chest rises and falls in quick succession and I have to lean over, bracing my hands on my knees.

"Stand up, cow," the guard that brought me out barks, but I ignore him. Did they track the other women too? God, I wish our plan had worked.

"Through a little bioengineering help, we just pushed her into her designation, right to the peak of perfection. She's entering Estrus now. Her first cycle."

There's a round of approving murmurs and I can hear excitement in their voices. It makes me sick. The alien announcer is basically telling them I was picked at peak freshness. It reminds me of those grocery store tags meant to entice shoppers to buy frozen veggies, or the canned green beans nobody wants.

"You figured out how to make an Omega? How?" Another voice asks. It's airy and light, but like the first voice it sounds like it's coming from another room.

"That's a trade secret," the announcer demures, and I want to hit him. "Now, for such a prize as an Omega, what shall we start the bidding at? Remember, this Omega is entering her first Estrus cycle, and that is a rare delicacy to be enjoyed by only those with the utmost...stamina."

Bile rises in my throat and I raise my hand to cover my mouth. I have to concentrate on breathing to not get sick all over the stage at that last word. *Stamina.* I might not know what Omega means, or Estrus, but I know it's not good. Not when it comes to me being sold to one of these faceless aliens. There is no doubt in my mind that once I'm bought and paid for they'll do whatever they want with me.

"100,000 credits," the raspy voice calls out.

"150,000 credits," the airy one shoots out, and from there it's a bidding war. I can't keep track of the numbers, they're being shouted so fast now. ***400,000, 420,000, 800,000***, is it a million now? I don't know. All I can do is stand there and try not to faint.

The announcers and the guards couldn't be happier. I can see their excitement with every bid for me. But all of that comes to a screeching halt when a shaft of light and the deafening sound of a door being jerked off its hinges fill the air. The sound of metal screeching as it's yanked out of its socket stops the bidding war.

"Halt! Halt right there!" The announcer shouts, doing his best to look in control of the situation, but I can tell he isn't. He's scared. Good. I hope he's terrified when this is all over. I don't even care if a three headed monster just walked in this joint, intent on wrecking it, and me. I just want the announcer to feel what I'm feeling.

Scared.

There's a growl and my knees go weak, nearly dropping out from under me. I stumble and manage to stay upright, but just barely, sweat slicked hands going to brace against my knees. I squint, trying to see who it is that's speaking, but the overhead lights are too bright. They cast everything but the stage in shadow. It's pitch black out there. It could be another frog alien for all I know.

"She's mine."

The scent of rain and citrus, so clean and refreshing that it chases away the sterile smell of the ship and whatever they blasted me with earlier. I take a deep breath and a moan comes out of my mouth. God, it smells so good. Delicious. Pure. Exactly what I want.

"*Mmmm.*" The sound is out of my mouth before

I can stop it. That's twice in just as many seconds that I've moaned for whoever is out there. I know it's them that I'm smelling. It has to be. When I feel the rumbling of another approving moan, I shove my hands over my mouth before I make any other sound that implies I'm remotely into this.

I should not be into this. *I am not into this.*

"You know the rules, Ryat! You bid from the station like everyone else. No one is aboard but us! These are the auction rules."

"She is mine." The growl is there again and it goes straight to my toes. I want to be his. I need to be his. My body is moving on it's own. I need to be closer to him. I need to hear him say that I'm his again. *Mine.* That word reverberates around in my head until it's all I can hear. My body knows exactly what it's hearing. I would know it even without the help of the language chip implant.

"Do you think you can keep what belongs to me away from me?"

Holy shit. I'm into this. I am so into this.

"Get my mate out of those cuffs and off that stage."

The pitch and timbre of his voice is low even though he's still hidden in the shadowy room. I take a step forward, edging closer to the edge of the stage and inhale again. He growls and I don't know if it's because I moved or because he wants to rip the announcer's head clean off. Whichever it is, I want more of that sound just as badly as I need more of this scent. It's like a balm to the suddenly stuffy room, breaking up the oppressive heat bubbling up from inside of me. I can breathe again, the tense set of my shoulders relaxing in spite of the scenario. I don't care what's going on. I want to see the man that's speaking.

"Leave at once, Ryat! You have no invitation to be here." The announcer flings a webbed hand towards the guard. "Get him out of here."

The guard swallows hard. His hand is shaking, the shock stick he'd threatened me with earlier isn't looking so steady now, and I smile. "But he's Ryat the Destroyer."

I don't a lot about this new world I'm in, but I know **Ryat the Destroyer** sounds scary as hell. I'd be shaking too.

"Get him out of here."

The guard croaks in fear. The sound of it makes me happy, because he's scared. I want him scared. I want them all scared. *"But he's a Royal Alpha."* There's a slight whine in his voice and I hear the unspoken words there. *If you want him out of here, you do it.* He's scared shitless, and I know he isn't going to fight.

What is a Royal Alpha? It has to be connected with whatever it is that the frog aliens are calling me. Omegle? Omnia?

"*Omega,*" Ryat the Destroyer grits out, his voice rough and deep like gravel rolling underfoot. Instantly, my eyes move to where I think he's standing. *Omega.* That was it! I snap my sweaty fingers and smile despite my predicament.

"What's an Omega?" I ask, but no one answers me. Everyone, or *every-alien,* is focused on Ryat. I guess that's what happens when your name is followed by 'Destroyer.' "What the hell is a Royal Alpha?" I ask, but Ryat's talking again and all the focus is right on him.

"Get my mate off that stage, frog," Ryat snarls. He's walking, I can hear his footsteps echoing in the room. It doesn't sound like anyone's standing in his way, even though I can hear voices protesting his sudden appearance. *"That is a royal order."* Again, the rumble of a growl that makes me think of the time I saw the lions at the Zoo, or in live-streams when I couldn't sleep. It's a low sound, the kind that reminds you that you are in the presence of a predator. That even if there's an enclosure, or the safety of the internet, between you and them, things would be very different if you were even a little bit closer.

I watch the announcer's webbed hand shake. There are no safety enclosures here.

"Why is Ryat there?!"

"You said we had to bid from the station!"

"This is unprofessional."

The voices from the darkness are ringing in the room. Bouncing off the walls and floor, getting louder with each complaint, but I don't hear anyone moving. Not until Ryat moves. I know it's him, the heavy footfall on the floor accompanied with a fresh wave of rainwater. It can't be anyone else but him. He's coming closer to me.

Thank god. *I need him.*

Ryat doesn't answer, just keeps right on walking up to the stage. Footstep after slow footstep. I know any second now he'll come into view. I can't see him, but I can sense him. He can't be more than a few feet off the stage, just outside of my field of vision. I'm shaking now, but not from fear like the frog guard in front of me. He's trying to look tough, but it isn't working. He raises his lighting stick. It crackles, growing brighter, when he speaks.

"Stay back," he orders.

"You have 30 seconds to leave this ship," the

announcer bellows, but his hands are still shaking and he's edging back from where he'd been standing before. He's no longer by the front of the stage, but slowly making his way towards the exit.

I hear a chuckle from the audience. "I'll leave when I have my Omega," he says. "Give me my mate."

Omega. There's that word again. I wish I knew what it meant, and why the hell I want to be with this Ryat the Destroyer. And all because he smells good? But how can I even smell him from here? God, why is my skin itchy and hot? It's like my clothes are too rough, the fabric scratching my skin and making it prickle. I suck in another breath. Ryat's scent fills my nose. He smells like heaven. The wetness between my legs grows and I shift, trying to ignore the fact that I don't just feel sick anymore.

I'm horny.

I wrap my arms around my chest and sway on my feet, eyes still off stage but when I move towards the edge again the frog guard turns to me. Fuck! Why am I horny? Of all the times, it picks now? My libido has been in the gutter for months. I think before I knew Ben was cheating on me, my body sensed it. I haven't wanted him in my bed for weeks now. My soul knew before I did. It knew then, just like it knows now.

Mate.

That word. I know what it means, even if I'm clueless about Omegas and Alphas. I know Ryat is claiming me as his. His mate. His Omega. His. His. *His.* A mate isn't just for rutting, though you wouldn't know it with the way my body is feeling, aching and practically screaming for this Ryat.

"Back up, cow," he snaps, waving the lighting stick at me. The crackling white end of it comes close to me, the heat of it warms my face and snaps me right out of the need to get closer to the Royal Alpha.

There's the sound of quick steps, and then a deafening roar. It makes me think of all the Nat-geo footage of lions and tigers. Predators that rend their prey to shreds under the weight of their claws and teeth. I stumble back, but it's not from fear. I'm not like the frogs. I'm not scared of the roar. My mind is on something else. It's on the fact that I have to get out of my clothes. I lift my cuffed hands and pull at my top. It's sticking to me now. I'm sweating and I didn't even realize it, but now I feel it. My skin is hot and feverish. Oh, no, am I sick? How am I getting sick this fast? I'm achy and I wince, moving my hands across my sternum. I fall back, ass hitting the floor with a thump.

Ryat the Destroyer, *Royal Alpha at large*, lands on the edge of the stage with the flash of a sword. He's carrying a sword. I stare at it, confused. Who carries swords anymore? But then again, I'm in a spaceship, so who am I to judge what kind of weapons a man uses. And he is a man. I feel the anxiety in my chest lessen slightly at seeing that Ryat looks no different than me. He's a man. There are no webbed fingers, or green, slightly slimy skin. He's human. Or at least, I think he is. This man is massive, tall. Taller than any man I've ever seen, and he looks like every fitness influencer, movie superhero, or what I think the male human form looks like after a round of photoshop.

Ryat is *built*. Built like a damn brick house. He has dark hair, the kind that I know was probably once combed neatly at the start of the day, but now is falling forward over his eyes. He has full lips, a straight and strong nose, high cheekbones, and a jaw that could cut glass. My eyes rake over his face. His too beautiful, but somehow also savage, face. With eyes so dark they look black. He has to be the prettiest man I've ever seen outside of an airbrushed fashion spread.

He's wearing leather pants?

No, they're breeches if I was going to try and describe what I was seeing. Bless whatever space god made those pants, because they are clinging to his body like they were poured right on him. Thick, muscular, thighs give way to a narrow waist and damn...this man is barrel chested. My eyes move up past the sight of his leather pants to see Ryat is wearing armor. There are thick glistening buckles inset into leather straps across his chest that I see holds up a sort of partial-plated armor that covers his arm and shoulder. A crimson cape falls from his shoulders and nearly hits the floor. I fixate on the red material. He's calling me his mate. A man with a cape is calling me his mate. Not just a man, but a devastatingly gorgeous man they call 'the Destroyer,' is here for me.

Me.

He charges forward, cape swirling around him, sword flashing beneath the stage lights. He points his sword at the guard that just swung at me. "Touch my mate and I'll take your head."

The frog makes another frightened sound and the lightning stick drops to the ground with a clatter. "I-I-" the guard starts, but the announcer interrupts, hopping around and screaming.

The announcer waves his hands. "Fight him! Get him out of here!" he orders. "The Omega isn't for sale unless it's done through the auction."

"He's Ryat. *You* fight him!" The guard yells back at the announcer.

"I need to lay down," I rasp, but no one is paying attention to me. No one is paying attention to Ryat, or the announcer who is now locked in a standoff. Not even the nervous guard. You'd think those three would be enough to keep eyes off of me, but the reason no one pays me any mind is because out of the back, the women are rushing the stage.

"Let her go, you frog asshole!" Sally screams, out front and leading the charge. She runs straight into the guard in front of me, shoving him off the stage with one well placed kick. Holy shit. She Spartan kicked the frog into next week.

Rose is right there too, and she hits the announcer so hard his tablet flies out of his hand and smashes to the floor. "Guards!" He screams on the way down, and I know this isn't great. We're about to have company.

I wobble trying to get up to help, but I'm weak. The ache inside of me is worse. It's not just my skin that's hot anymore. My insides feel like they're on fire.

"What do we do?" Rose cries when she catches sight of me. "She looks sick!"

"I don't know, I thought it would-" Sally begins, but there are more frog guards. They're running up behind us, their glowing sticks charged and ready to rumble.

"*Run*," I rasp. I wave a hand, gesturing towards the light still pouring in from the entrance this Ryat, the Royal Alpha guy, made. "Out that way. *Go!*"

Sally is the first to react. She turns towards me and bends to wrap an arm around my waist. "Not without you."

"I'm sick," I tell her with a shake of my head. "Leave me." I'm just going to slow them down. They have to leave me behind if they are going to make it out of here before the guards arrive. The door into the room is open now, they could run right out of here and no one could stop them.

"No!" Sally screams, her arms going tighter around me. She gives me a hard yank, but I don't really move and instead I slump forward, hands on the floor. She feels bad about before. That's why she ran out here. But now the plan is shit, because I don't know what's in front of us. I can hear Ryat growling, the sound of him hitting the guard echoes, and a second later the limp body of the guard sails through the air and lands on the stage with a skip and a thud. The announcer is trying to run from him, I think. I see a webbed hand rise and grip the side of the stage, the newly arrived guards yell, their feet stomping as they rush up the stairs.

"Run." I'm weak, my hair is stuck to my forehead, strands plastered to my cheeks. I give Sally as hard of a push as I can muster. "Get out of here. Take the others."

"No." She's fierce, but I'm tired. So tired and hot and aching. My body needs something, anything, to relieve the pain starting to take over. I clench my thighs without thinking and shudder at the feel of my pants. The too tight and too itchy material is suddenly giving me the friction I need. I can feel myself getting wet. *Oh god*. What alien plague did I pick up that I'm getting horny in the middle of a fight? I thought earlier it was a one off. Maybe my fight or flight system confused my body into thinking it's horny. But no, here it is again.

I blink, trying to clear the sweat now burning my eyes. I look up, but my vision is blurry. It doesn't matter how much I wipe my eyes or blink. It's like a haze, a rosy haze that's settling over everything, casting the world in a pink tint. I try to stand, but my knees give out and I hit the ground, landing right back where I started with a moan. My hands are no help, arms shaking and refusing to hold my weight when I try to sit up.

Sally won't let me go. Her hands are slipping on my sweat slicked skin, but she tries to haul me up anyways. Bless this woman. Even though she was too scared before, she's refusing to back down now. I think we're surrounded. It feels like we're surrounded by the guards. I can see the shapes of the other woman, all of them bunched up around me. I'm on the floor at the center of women facing off the frog guards. "Grab her, we have to-"

"*Omega.*"

My body shudders at that one word. A sound I've never heard before rips out of me, the keen of it vibrating low in my throat before ending in a high pitched whine. Why do I sound like that? My body is hurting, aching, and when Sally tries to come near me again, I hear the deep growl of the man that barged in here.

The one calling me his.

Ryat the Destroyer.

"Omega."

My hands go down on the floor and I hold myself there for a beat before I'm struggling in Sally's grasp. I don't want her touching me. I thrash my limbs, trying to get free. She smells wrong. Her hands aren't right. I want the rain. I want the scent of citrus on my skin. I want, I want... *I want...*

"*Alpha!*" I cry out and flail, trying to get closer. But it's all wrong. There are too many people here. The smells are making me sick. I can smell the frogmen, the guards with their slightly sour stench that makes me want to cover my mouth. The women are overwhelming, too sweet, too floral, their scent is overpowering, especially mixed with fear like it is. I don't want to be scared. I don't want to be near the announcer's smell of acidic anger, so strong I can taste it on my tongue.

I flinch when I feel someone touch me. Their hands are too rough on me. This is not the one I want. *The Alpha.* That's who I want. Who my body needs. The pink haze colors everything I see. I blink rapidly and try to regain focus, but it's no use. Everything moves like I'm seeing it through a misted over mirror. I can make out the shapes, the sizes, but I need him. He's close. But even close is achingly far away when it's not where I can touch him.

"Alpha," I try again. *"Alpha."* I shove away from the person holding me and crawl forward, head bent low and to the side, exposing my neck. I don't know...

I don't know why I'm doing it, but it feels right. I want him to see how submissive I am.

"Alpha, please," I beg. I've never begged for anything in my life, but here I am on the floor, begging in front of a room full of people and aliens. I don't care. I'll do anything if he comes to me.

Anything.

He comes closer, vaulting onto the stage. The thud of his booted feet hitting the floor makes a vibration so great I feel it in my palms and thighs. The guards scatter back. They're scared. I can smell it. Their fear makes me happy. I smile and reach out my arms for the Alpha stalking closer to me.

"Darcy, no!" Sally is trying to hold me back. "Not him!"

"Maybe we should..." Rose's voice is there and then it trails off, because he's here now. In front of me. *Finally.* I fall forward, hands and face pressed close to his feet. I scoot close to his legs and pull myself close, clinging to him. My wrists are still cuffed so it makes holding on to him hard but I manage it. I can't let anyone take me from him. I'll die if they do. The heat in my body spikes, and I know it's true. If he doesn't fix this, no one will be able to do it.

"It hurts," I gasp. My fingers scrabble at his legs,

there's heavy plating there across his shins and it's cold to the touch beneath my hands, but it doesn't do anything to break the fever I have. I press my forehead to his grieves. "It hurts, it hurts, it hurts," I sob. The sounds coming out of me are weak and pitiful. I almost don't recognize them as my own, but my throat is sore from it, my cheeks are stained wet from my tears. They land on the floor beside Ryat's feet. His hand is in my hair, the weight of it calming me slightly. It soothes me, and I lean into his touch. I whimper when I feel him card his fingers through the strands.

He slowly combs his hand through my hair, fingers tugging lightly on the ends before he moves to do it again. A happy sigh escapes my lips and I cling harder to him, pressing my cheek to his thigh. If I was in my right mind I'd be embarrassed at what I look like. I'm on my knees, horny as hell, while this man pets me. There's no other word for what he's doing. His hand moves through my hair again and the light drag of his fingertips against my scalp confirms it. Yup, he's 10000% petting me. I nuzzle my cheek into him, getting as close as I can while he touches me, because I'm not in my right mind and I don't give a shit what I look like right now as long as this man keeps running his hands through my hair.

I see the glint of his sword come into view out of the corner of my eye. He's not in any hurry. Staring them all down with a sword in one hand, while he pets me with his other. He moves, nudging me back from him slightly, and I whine at the distance. But it's only after his sword whistles through the air between us and slices through the cuffs I'm wearing that I understand. I'm not even phased when the cuffs fall to the ground with a clatter and his sword comes to rest beside me once more. I just scramble to throw my arms around his legs and press my face against his thigh again.

What the hell kind of universe is this? Whatever it is, I know it definitely isn't mine.

"How much for my mate?" Ryat's voice is nice. I really like it, and I wish he'd keep speaking. Anything to not listen to the frogs.

"One million credits." I frown when I hear the announcer. I don't like him. I want my Alpha's voice in my ears.

"I should kill you for taking her from me. And now this price?"

"We made her. We didn't take her. The price is fair, even for a Royal Alpha."

I want to lift my head to look up at my Alpha, but if I did I'd have to move away from the hand stroking my head. I try to remember what he looks like, but it's hard. Thinking...it's all getting to be hard. I know he's big, that he smells right, that my body needs him. But the haze, it's hard to focus. All I am is a ball of heat and need. The wet spot between my legs is bigger now, I know there's no hiding it, but I don't care. I hold onto the Alpha tighter and duck my head.

There's a scream and a crash. I hear a monitor hit the ground and glass skitters across the floor before another bang sounds. Another screen is broken, and the announcer sighs.

"One million *five hundred*."

"I'll have it transferred."

He bends down, picks me up, and turns back towards the door he just tore open. My head lolls to the side and I see the women I came here with standing off the stage. They are in the space that was once blacked out. There's rows and rows of screens, some of them are black, but there are angry faces on some too. They aren't happy with what's happened.

They wanted to win the auction. The auction for me, and I shiver. I don't want any of them. I only want him. I turn, burying my nose into his neck, the scent of rain calming me enough that the haze is pushed back. My brain isn't so fogged up now. He drops down from the platform, but I don't feel the impact. It's smooth, just like his gait out of the room.

I frown. Something's wrong. The air is heavy with an acrid stench. Like burning sulfur. It makes my eyes water. I look back, the women are staring after me. Some are crying. It's not from the smell though. The smell is them. They're scared. Terrified.

"No," I say, raising a hand to his shoulder. "Stop."

He stops immediately. Dark eyes meet mine, I see a sharp nose, the high bridge of it leading to those dark eyes that are now considering me. Eyes so dark they're nearly black. "No," I say again and raise a shaky hand to point at the women behind us. "Take them too."

His lip raises in a snarl. He doesn't like that idea, but I don't care. I can't leave them. "Alpha," I breathe, leaning closer. "*Please*. Save them." He goes still, his strong jaw clenching and unclenching as he thinks. I take in another deep breath and he does the same. We breathe together, inhale and exhale, the rise and fall of our chests in sync. His eyes drift closed and his face softens. He opens his eyes to look at me.

"This is what you want, little Omega?"

I nod. I still don't know what an Omega is, but it

is important to him. That means I'm important to him. I have to be, if I'm his mate. I can tell he wants to please me. He lets out a long exhalation when I nod and then says, "I'm taking the rest of the humans."

"You can't! It took us ages to collect them all!" The announcer erupts. My Alpha goes still, turns, and levels a stare at the frogs.

"I'll take your heads instead if you would rather."

"It's another million, and you have a deal."

My Alpha grunts in acquiesce. The announcer curses. He thought my Alpha was bluffing, and I smile. Stupid frog. I wish he was scared again. He inhales deeply, slit nostrils expanding slightly, before he motions for the women to follow after us. "Take your cows and leave."

CHAPTER 4

There's a scramble of activity and the women run after us with excited whoops, but I can't focus anymore. A cramp wracks me, my stomach clenches, and I cry out. It hurts again. The smell of my Alpha isn't helping anymore. We're moving again.

The arms that hold me go tight around me and then his lips are by my ear. "Shhh, Omega."

"It hurts," I whine and cling to him.

"I know, little Omega."

"Please."

He doesn't answer me but he does growl. Or purr? It's a rumble in his chest that I like. It sounds so good and it helps me focus on something other than the cramps. I relax in his arms even though I'm sweating again. The steady rumble of his chest beneath my palms feels right. I snuggle closer to him and an answering purr passes my lips. My Alpha likes that. I can tell from his smell. The citrus of him is like sunshine. He's pleased.

I purr louder, doing my best to make him even happier.

"What's with the sounds?" a woman asks.

"Shhh, it's a mating ritual," another woman answers. "She's in heat."

It's quiet after that. Just the sound of my Alpha's rumble in my ears. There's a whoosh and doors open and shut behind us several times before we're somewhere new. It smells better here. Not sterile, not sour, there's no anger in the air, or fear. That scent is quickly fading from the women with us.

This smells right. It smells like my Alpha.

I hear a murmur of voices and then the women are gone. The haze is back stronger than ever and everything feels fuzzy, like in a dream. Maybe I was dreaming all along? The sudden thought manages to puncture through the haze I'm in and I realize I'm in a set of rooms. These are nice rooms that look lived in. It's not the cold gleaming metal of the frog's ship. There are rugs on the floor and there's a bed at the center of it. We're alone.

Am I still dreaming? Is that what happened? Will I wake up from this and be back with Ben?

I feel sick again, but it's not from the thought that I'm lost in space with a man I don't know. A man I've been calling 'Alpha.' Or the fact that I'm beyond horny. He is still holding me close, the wetness between my legs now a slow trickle. There's too much of it. This isn't right.

Except that…it feels right. It feels so completely perfect, that the thought of losing this man makes me want to scream. I keen, the low sound of it distraught and strangled in my throat. Instantly, my Alpha growls. Not a purr, but a growl. He's looking for a threat, but I don't know how to tell him that the only threat I feel is losing him. His eyes that I thought were dark before are slowly darkening more, the pupil of them blown wide, overtaking the whites of his eyes. I raise a hand to touch him and the slight brush of my fingers against his cheek stops the growl. We stare at one another and then a fresh wave of pain hits me. But that isn't the only thing that I feel.

Arousal. I need him. I need his cock. It's the only thing that's going to fix the ache inside of me.

"Please," I whisper again. The haze is there, pulling at the edges of my vision. It won't fall, not completely. The whispering thought that I might wake from this distresses me so much I can't give into the haze. Not fully. My Alpha moves towards the bed, the softness of it at my back relaxes me slightly. He's settling himself above me, hands starting to move over my body, petting me, soothing away the aches with each drag of his rough fingers. The haze gets heavier, the pink starting to fill in my reality.

I can let go, it tells me. Have this. Let my Alpha take me. Claim me, and it'll all feel better.

"Let me make it better, little Omega." He kisses my neck and I gasp at the first brush of his lips on my skin. My body bucks, my hips push off the bed seeking more of my Alpha. He can make it better, my brain starts to chant. He can make it better, he can, *he can*.

I don't know how I know this, but it's the only sane thought in my brain. I'm letting the haze move in, heavy and thick. I don't care about anything. There was something I was worried about, but it's not important anymore. Not with my Alpha starting to pull my clothes off. They smell like the place from before, like the beady eyed things that I hate. I want my clothes off of me now desperately. I raise my arms and let him take my top off, throwing it towards the corner of the room. I sigh and settle back onto the bed. It's soft under me, but it isn't soft enough. There aren't enough blankets and pillows.

I move away and the distance pulls a growl from my Alpha. A warning. He doesn't like me moving away. He wants me close, but it doesn't matter. I want more pillows, more softness, there needs to be more on the bed. I want a pile of blankets and pillows to mold and shape. My skin feels tight, like there are a thousand bees beneath my skin, humming and buzzing angrily. The energy of it has me vibrating and squirming. I need my Alpha to touch me, but before he can do that I have to build...I have to build *something*.

A nest.

The thought comes to me. The word pops into my brain before I can register it. I can see exactly how I want it. Blankets and pillows all formed together into a snug place. A safe place. I sink down in the haze. Pink tinges my vision, but I see the way my Alpha's eyes are nearly black from his blown pupils. My eyes probably look exactly the same. He touches my neck, fingers curving around the base, his palm pressing into the soft curve of my neck. I come towards him, letting him guide me where he wants. His free hand is at the top of my pants, and he jerks the top button free. I shiver when I hear the whisper soft ***zzr rht*** sound of my zipper being pulled down.

I try to move to help him, but my Alpha's grip on my neck tightens and I freeze. He's so much bigger than me, so keeping a hold on me and pulling my pants free is done in seconds. I tilt my head back to look up at him when he steps closer. I'm naked now. I can feel the warm leather of his pants pressing against my overheated skin. I moan as I scoot closer to him and try to push my hips against his. His other hand comes up to fist in my hair. He doesn't pet me like he did before. Now his grip is strong.

He yanks my head back and I whine at the rough touch, but I obey, my head falling back and to the side. I'm baring my neck to him. Showing him he's in charge. From the guttural moan of approval I hear rumbling from him, he's happy with it. So am I. Or at least, I am when he forces one thick thigh between my legs. I almost sob in relief when I feel the first press of his warm bulk against my aching cunt. I grind down on him, roll my hips and moan while he holds me. His hand on my neck is tense, fingers digging into my skin, and when he tugs my head back further I hiss in pain. A moment later the hiss turns into a moan of pleasure. The slick between my legs is dripping, getting all over his thigh in a wet sticky mess—and god does it feel fucking fantastic.

I roll my hips faster, rubbing my clit against his leg as he rocks into me, adding just a little extra punch to my efforts. This goes on for maybe another half a minute before I scream, an orgasm rolling through me before I go limp against his broad chest. I feel the tip of his nose against my neck. He's scenting me. The warm puff of his breath against my sensitive skin makes me shiver, but I keep still, letting him move me towards the bed. He sets me down and I see I've made a mess of the both of us. My thighs and pussy are wet, just like his thigh I rode, but he doesn't seem to mind it. I watch him drop a hand to his thigh. The slick there shines under the lights of the room and he runs a thick finger through it. A second later he raises his finger to his lips and dips it into his mouth.

I swallow hard when I hear him hum in approval at the way I taste. Those full lips set in that face confuses me. Sensuality surrounded by raw rugged features. He takes his finger out of his mouth and moves close, extending his still wet finger to me. I lean forward, sucking it into my mouth without a second thought. I taste myself and my Alpha, the musky, heady, taste of my own cum mixed with his skin. I swirl my tongue over the pad of his finger, licking it clean. I feel his free hand fist in the material of the hoodie I'm still wearing.

A low growl sounds from him before he has a knife in his hand and quickly cuts the seam on the side of my hoodie, yanking it off of me. I'm still sucking his finger when he cuts my top and bra off in one clean motion. I'm naked now, but the cool air of the room does nothing against my overheated body. My Alpha moves his finger from my mouth and I let it go with a little pop of my lips.

The orgasm took the edge off and I can think enough to know I have one thing left to do before I take my Alpha's cock.

"Wait," I get out, but it's difficult. "Wait," I whisper again. Soon I won't be able to form words. Just speaking the one was hard enough, when all I want to do is throw myself in his arms and beg him to fuck me. What did they call it? Estrus? Rose said it was a heat. *God*. That's exactly how I feel. My body is hotter than it was during the auction, the wetness between my thighs is too much. I'm grateful for the relief he gave me, but I need more. The emptiness inside of me is growing once more until my pussy is dripping and aching for the Alpha in front of me. The scent of my arousal is heavy in the air, filling the space all around us. I hear my Alpha inhale deeply. His mouth is open when he sucks in another lungful of my scent. I whine and feel another gush of wetness between my legs. There's too much for this to be normal. It's the heat. The Estrus that has me keyed up and aching for my Alpha. He's the only one that can fix this. He smells good. Strong, healthy, virile. I know he can fix this. Can fix me.

And there's only one way to fix the pain rolling through my body.

I need a cock in my cunt, and teeth in my neck.

The thought is fully-formed in my mind even if speaking is too much. I can feel my instincts taking over. Instincts that I didn't even know I had in me. It's like my body has been hijacked, operating on some new autopilot, and I'm just in the passenger seat observing. Whatever the aliens pumped me full of, the biological nudge they were talking about that forced me into whatever an Omega is, it's speaking to me now. Perfectly honed into the frequency of my deepest instinctual urges. I know sex with my Alpha will take away all the pain. I know I need his teeth marking me, bonding me to him, and I want it. My grasp on lucidness slips further and further away with every second that ticks by. I whine, my words lost to me. There's only need and instinct. Whatever it is that's in me has changed how I operate.

He reaches for me again and I dodge his hands and yank at the sheets. I pull them off the bed, make them into a ball, and shove a pillow and then another into the mass I made.

It's not right. I need more.

I take apart the pillows I have. Yank the sheets free and try to rearrange them again, but I can only manage half of what I want. No, less than half. There isn't enough here to make a proper nest. I need somewhere I can feel safe. Warm, protected, cozy and comfortable, while I take my Alpha's fat cock.

I move up to my knees, a keen high in my throat when I feel him at my back. He's warm, his bulk solid and comforting. The sound I'm making dwindles and then he's purring. That low sound makes me go quiet. I turn to him and see him putting an armful of blankets near me. They smell like him, so I purr happily and grab the blankets. They have good bulk, their lush softness beneath my hands makes me giddy. This is what I need. I start arranging them, fully distracted when he puts down a stack of pillows beside me. These pillows are not like the first two I used. Those were utilitarian. More for comfort and everyday use than anything else. Dark gray and solid in their construction. Spartan.

No frills, no comfort, nothing unnecessary.

The pillows he's putting down now are anything but utilitarian. These pillows are soft and pastel colored. They're soft to the touch, some of them are almost velvet. The smooth material slides beneath my palms when I run my hands over the overstuffed pillows.

I purr. My Alpha makes a sound of approval. He's pleased that I'm happy. Of course I'm happy. He's here, and my nest is being put to rights. I have my Alpha. I'm secure and happy. The heat isn't so painful anymore. Not with him nearby. The longer he's close to him the more my body relaxes. His scent is a reassuring reminder that I will not be alone for my heat. I will be mated, the hunger and heat inside of me fed completely. When I have my nest put together, I reach back and grab his hand.

"Alpha," I groan and give his hand a firm tug. He comes forward easily. Lets me pull him with me. I push him back onto the bed and then begin to work at removing his armor, but the straps and buckles are confusing to me. I struggle for a second more before he nudges my hand aside and takes over. I watch impatiently, but he's quick. His cape and armor are discarded to the side of the bed, his pants, grieves, and boots follow quickly before he's just as naked as me. I surge forward and wrap my arms around him. I bury my face into his neck and smile, licking his skin. He tastes delicious. I drop my hand to touch his big cock. It's easily the largest I've ever seen, but that might be because he's the largest man I've ever seen. Nearly twice my size. Our difference in frames is highlighted now that we are in bed and close like this, even to my haze heavy brain. I move my hand up and down his thick length. My fingers can't close around it, but I try anyway. I lean close and drag my tongue across the head of it, but before I can take him in my mouth he stops me with a hand fisting in my hair.

My Alpha groans and the sound goes straight to my clit. I'm wet, wetter than I've ever been. Slick is pooling, wetting my thighs and I lick my lips, straining to get closer to him. It's impossible to move since he's still holding me still by my hair.

"*Alpha*," I rasp again, and he moves, taking charge then. My clit throbs, the earlier orgasm he gave me is already forgotten as the razor sharp edge of my heat descends on me again.

"You're mine, little Omega. Be still." He lifts my head up, bringing my face to his and captures my mouth in a bruising kiss. He pushes me back where he wants me until I sit in front of him. His fingers twist roughly in my hair. He pulls my head and forces me nearly onto my back. My neck is exposed like this, and I feel the skin at the base of my neck, right where my shoulder meets it, heat. It throbs, and my pulse jumps. It's where he'll mark me. My body lights right up at the thought, the soft juncture of skin practically glows, showing my Alpha the easiest way to bond me.

I whimper. I want him.

I want whatever he deigns to give me, and so I wait. I work to hold myself steady and still while he begins to explore my body. He moves, trailing a nose up the column of my exposed neck. I swallow hard and try to relax into his hold. It hurts, the way he's holding me, so that the crown of my head touches the bed. The arch of my neck makes it hard to swallow, but I know why he's doing it. He wants me to relax, to go pliant in his hands, but my body needs him.

I fidget, losing the battle with myself, and push my hips towards him. He nips my throat, teeth sharp on my skin but not breaking the skin. It's a warning bite. But still, I try to push my hips up to him. I can feel his big cock against my leg. I'm breathless and shivering, aching for more, when he says, "You get what I give you. You belong to me." He moves and buries a hand in my hair. He twists the strands around his fingers, yanking back on my locks, holding my head so that my throat is exposed to him. His other hand goes to my stomach.

"You are mine, little Omega."

His.

I'm his. We both know it.

There's no other reason why he would have me here. I've submitted to him, baring my neck, giving him a soft place to mark me. It's the way an Omega should be when her Alpha is nearby. He noses further down, lips and teeth grazing my collar bone before he captures a nipple in his mouth. The hot wet swipe of his tongue across my sensitive skin makes me tremble, but I refuse to move.

My Alpha told me not to move so I won't do it. Not until his cock is buried in me. Not until...not until...my brain goes foggy.

I want something from him. I don't know what it is, but my body knows. I clench my pussy, it's empty and I hurt. I want my Alpha inside of me. Buried deep in my cunt. I want his teeth in my neck when he claims me and fills me with his cum, but there's nothing.

I'm empty, and the pain is back.

The ache inside of me is growing by the nanosecond. I gasp when a sharp pain shoots through my body. I shake, a shudder rolling through me. I move my head to the side and a sob escapes my lips. My Alpha coos, the purr no longer enough to stop me.

He doesn't like that I'm in pain.

I know he doesn't by the way he moves between my thighs, parting them with his massive frame. He's almost twice my size and the weight of him pressing me into the bed feels euphoric. My skin was starving for him. I know that when the too tight feeling vanishes from it. Only my aching pussy is left, the pain of it coming to life again in me. But I know my relief is close. He's where I need him, between my thighs, filling my nest, poised to rut me. He has his cock in hand and the first delicious slide of his cock through my wet folds nearly makes me scream. I suck in a breath, prepared to endure his teasing, but then he surprises me.

He grips my hips, takes them roughly in his hands, and moves me. He flips me onto my stomach, the flat of his palm pressing between my shoulder blades, pushing my body into the mattress and blankets beneath me. I try to push up onto my hands, but he's stronger than me and keeps me where I am while he hooks an arm beneath my hips, lifting me onto my knees where he wants me. My ass is in the air, chest pressed to the bed under the weight of his hand between my shoulder blades.

I whine, a low keen that's desperate for him, but I don't have to wait long before I feel the blunt head of his cock between my legs. His head slides through my slick wet folds and I sob, the raw sound ripped from my throat. I feel warmth at my back when he comes forward, presses his chest to my spine, and covers me. I whine again, wanting him to fuck me but he growls and the sound reminds me to be patient.

To wait.

He noses at my neck and then lower still until I feel his lips brush over the most sensitive bit of flesh on my whole body. That place where my neck and shoulder meet. I shiver, but keep still.

He's going to mark me. Bond me as his.

I will be still because it's not just his lips on my skin, but his teeth. Teeth graze my skin in time with his cock nudging at my aching entrance. I feel the warm head of his cock start to ease into me at the same time as I feel his teeth sink into my neck. He bites me and thrusts into my pussy at the same moment.

"Alpha!" I cry out, and he bites me harder,

breaking the skin. He rolls his hips, the movement feeding me more of his length, and I sigh happily. His teeth are still in my neck as he gives me inch after thick inch of his cock. The stretch of him is painful, but it's the kind of pain that makes my blood sing. The ache of my empty cunt is no more, the pain of my heat is over, with his cock inside of me.

I mewl when I feel his hips press against my ass. He's fully seated in me. His big body is heavy over mine, keeping me still when my Alpha purrs for me. The low sound vibrates through my body, fills the air around us, and I go pliant in my Alpha's grip.

I'm safe and protected here.

The knowledge of it is bone deep. Nothing can touch me, hurt me, or take me from him. He will protect me with his dying breath. I know this. He starts to move then. His cock slides in and out of me, faster and faster with each stroke.

It isn't long before he's set a pace that is both brutal and not enough at the same time. When he bites down at my neck again, I come apart, orgasming so hard my breath comes in choking gasps and sobs. All through it my Alpha keeps fucking me. Thick cock filling and stretching my pussy, punishing my body with the force of his thrusts. But my body wants more. My body is primed for more.

It's only another minute before I come on his cock again.

"Alpha!" I scream out. I can feel his cock get larger. It's swelling now inside of me, getting thicker and thicker at the base and stretching my cunt even more.

He thrusts into me and I cry out when I feel the head of his cock stroke against the front wall of my cunt. It's sensitive, the nerves there responsive to the pressure my Alpha is applying there. He moves, rising up onto his knees, and I feel his hands once more on my back, fingers moving to dig into my shoulders while he continues to fuck into me. I come again on his cock, body pressed to the bed, fingers twisting in the sheets while I scream out my release.

I'm a mess, and I know I'm babbling. Incoherent words and whimper are streaming out of me. I beg for more. I beg for him to stop. I don't know which I mean, and neither does my body.

But my Alpha does.

He doesn't stop. My Alpha's thick cock is inside of me, buried deep, his warm bulk above me. He moves faster as I writhe beneath him, and I feel the base of his cock swell. It's larger than the rest of his length, and the growing knot at the base of his cock slides in and out of me. My pussy stretches over it and there is a sharp sting that turns into pleasure almost immediately. It feels so good that it almost pulls another orgasm from my body.

My Alpha gives another hard thrust into me. His cock is deep inside of me and he holds it there for a second before I feel the start of his cum filling me. He slides a hand into my hair and grips my hips, turning us onto our side, and pulls me tight to his chest. He shudders as the knot swells to capacity and locks our bodies together. I moan and push my hips back into my Alpha. The swollen knot of his cock is the ultimate cure for the ache in me. My pussy spasms and clenches down hard on my Alpha's fat knot.

I feel a stream of his cum fill me, and then another. Ropes of it shoot out, coating my insides. Painting my insides as his. The swollen base of his cock ensures every drop of cum stays inside of me. His hand slides from my hip to my belly, palm pressed flat to my skin, fingers splayed out possessively over my skin.

He's so close to me and he presses his nose to my neck, his teeth once more finding the mark he gave me. My skin breaks out in goosebumps when I feel his lips and tongue move over the fresh bite.

It feels like heaven.

I lean back into him and close my eyes. My body is tired and the pain of my heat is over. My Alpha took care of it. He's taking care of me now, holding me close, body curled to mine with his cock still buried in me. I'm safe. I can rest now.

I hear him inhale, the movement of his body moves me with him. I close my eyes and hear him speak. It's one word—*"Mine,"* rumbles low in my ear as I fall asleep.

CHAPTER 5

When I wake up it's quiet and I'm alone. The bed I'm in is not my own. *It's too...nice.* Too soft beneath me, the sheets and blankets around me lush. It smells good too. Too good to be my home and my bed.

I stretch across the bed, arms over my head and toes pointed. At home, I would have Ben's body taking up half the bed, including the blankets. It wasn't uncommon for me to wake up cold and with my legs half hanging off the mattress. It also didn't smell like this. It smelled like nothing, which I guess is weird when you think about home.

Home should smell like the things you love, but my home with Ben didn't smell like much other than whatever cleaning product I had used that day, or the generic plug in air-fresheners I picked up at the grocery store.

But that was probably because my "home," wasn't a home. It was just a house. A house that I paid for and shared with a man that didn't love or respect me. You can't make a house into a home, not when you share it with someone like that.

No, this isn't that. I have plenty of space here, and there's no shortage of blankets and pillows. All soft and luxurious.

I run a hand along the blanket beside me and press my nose to the material and inhale. It smells like things I love. The scent of rain and citrus. The clean crisp smell of it fills my nose and puts me at ease. I love this smell more than anything I scented in my house with Ben.

I rub my cheek against it and purr happily, but the sound is cut off abruptly when I realize what I'm doing.

"What the hell is this?" I whisper and sit up. "What am I doing?" I touch my throat and swallow hard. I've never made a sound like that before. I didn't even know I could. I can barely roll my R's when I order Carne Asada on Taco Tuesday, *let alone purr*.

I blink and try to get my bearings while I scan

the room. The room is low lit, the light in the space warm and comforting. I see weapons, sharp, shiny, glistening swords and knives hanging from the wall across from where I lay. I don't see any art on the walls. In fact, there's nothing on the walls except for the weapons. The only soft things in the room seem to be the pillows and blankets piled around me. The owner of this room is definitely into minimalism. Well, except for the weapons.

"Is that a scimitar?" I whisper. I crane my neck, taking in the curve of the blade that looks like something I saw once on a History Channel documentary series. Yup, it's definitely a scimitar.

The floor confuses me because it isn't wood, or tile, or any sort of treatment that I've ever seen on a floor before. It's almost metal? There's a dull sheen to it, but when I shimmy over to the edge of the bed and put a foot down it's not cold like you'd think metal would be. It's pleasantly warm. I wiggle my toes on the floor and go to stand but stop when I realize I'm naked.

This is normally when I, like any sane person who wakes up in a strange place naked, and on top of it all purrs, would panic. But I don't panic. I feel at peace with my current predicament. *I want to be here.* At least, I think I do? My memories are...*fuzzy*.

That's being generous considering the weird dreamy film that hits my memories like a social media filter turned up on high.

I suck in a deep breath and think. I concentrate on the series of events that brought me here and I wince, thinking of the frog aliens that abducted me. My hand goes to the spot below my ear when I remember the painful injection they gave me. I can feel a bump there, but nothing else. It feels completely healed over.

I run my fingers tentatively over the bump. There's no break in my skin. "Huh." I wouldn't think something like that would heal that fast, but I guess in space anything—my fingers freeze when more memories come to me. I remember another wound.

My neck.

My hand jerks to the space where my neck and shoulder meet. I can feel something there, but I can't see it. I look down but it's no dice. I can't see where the skin still feels tender. I stand quickly, jerk a sheet free from the pile on the bed, and wrap it around myself like a toga. It's not much, but the sheet is enough for me to consider myself sort-of-clothed and ready to explore. I cross the room to the only thing I see with a semi-reflective surface. The swords and knives wall.

I get close to the biggest of them all. Something that looks like it takes two people to lift. The blade is wider than my forearm, which makes it as good of a mirror as I'm going to get in this room. I lean close, bracing a hand on the wall, and squint at the reflection there. The metal is polished within an inch of its life, so what I see is relatively clear.

"Oh, fucking hell," I whisper when I spy the bite mark on my neck. It's perfectly formed and nearly healed from the looks of it. I run a finger along the sensitive skin.

"That fucker bit me. *He bit me*," I hiss. The fucker I'm talking about is now center stage in my trip down memory lane. I can see him stepping out of the darkness, terrible and beautiful all at the same time. I remember the feel of his arms around me as he carried me away from the auction and well...I also start to remember what it was that he did to me after he brought me here.

This room is his.

A door I hadn't noticed before slides open and speak of the devil. It's him. I know it's him without even looking away from my sword mirror. The smell of citrus and rainwater is stronger now. I suck in a deep breath, lips parting to better get it in my lungs, and I relax.

"My Alpha," I whisper.

"What are you doing out of bed?" His voice is low, gruff, but also soothing. There's a touch of a growl to it that I like. I feel it in my toes and I lift myself up on them slightly, trying to ground myself. I don't understand why I feel this way around him.

"I woke up," I reply and look over my shoulder at him. He's coming towards me, full lips in a frown. I move to push away from the wall, but I'm still on my toes so my hand slips slightly. That wouldn't normally be a big deal, but there is the teensy weensy little fact that I'm leaning against *a wall of swords*.

Quick as lightning, he's there beside me with a hand on my arm. He jerks me back from the wall with a disapproving growl.

"Get back in bed. *Now.*" There's a command there in the last word. I can feel it, heavy and hanging over me with all the force of a mack truck. I feel it so much, in fact, that my feet start moving before I can even register that I'm walking right back to the bed.

"Woah, why-" I begin, and then shake my head, my damn feet hot footing it to the bed before my traitorous legs climb right back in like I was told to do.

"Did you just make me do that?" I ask.

"Yes." He nods, crossing his arms and glaring at me. "You could have hurt yourself."

I'm silent for a second before I explode. "What the fuck?! You don't tell me what to do!"

His eyebrows lift in surprise. "I don't?" he asks, and now his mouth is pulling up into a smile.

I glare at him and his stupidly pretty mouth. "No. Absolutely not."

"Is that not our mark you carry?" he asks, starting to walk towards the bed.

"Now that you mention it, buddy." I flick a finger out at him. "We're going to talk about the fact that you bit me."

"Not bit. *Claimed*," he corrects. "I claimed you."

"Potato, poh-tah-toe," I tell him. "You put your teeth in my neck."

"I did."

"Why?"

"You're mine."

I blink. I hadn't expected him to say that. I don't know what I expected him to say, but it wasn't that. "What? What does that mean? I," I swallow and start again, "you can't just say someone's yours."

He doesn't speak, just comes to the side of the bed that I'm sitting on and stares down at me. We lock eyes, and for a second I try to keep my stare up, but damn, it's hard. I swallow and refuse to look away, or at least I do until I hear the warning rumble of a growl coming from him. Before I know it, my chin is down, pressed close to my chest. I frown and stare down at my lap where my hands are resting.

"I'm not surprised my mate is defiant," he says and runs a hand over my head, fingers light on my hair. He reaches behind me and lifts a braid I hadn't realized I was wearing, and drops it over my shoulder. I focus on the braid against my chest, it's in a pattern I've never seen before. Smaller braids of hair are woven together within a larger one. The effect is beautiful.

"Who made this braid?" I ask him, choosing to ignore the fact that he called me his mate. Or the fact that he just growled me into submission.

"I did," he says.

I lift my head slightly, but only manage to look at his collarbone. He's not wearing the armor I remember him in, but he's also not wearing normal clothing either. He's shirtless and sporting the leather style breeches I remember him in. It's a damn good look. I frown and stare at his chest, hating that he looks good enough to eat.

"Why?" I ask. "Why the braid, I mean?" Ben would have never thought to do my hair. The man hardly brought the groceries in, let alone braided my hair. Why would this sword obsessed Alpha braid my hair? Wait a second...

Alpha.

That's what the frogs kept calling him. It wasn't just the frogs that called him that. It's what *I* was calling him. My cheeks heat when the memories of what this man did to me for, god knows how long in this room, floods my mind. No, I didn't just call him that, I screamed it.

I screamed it until my voice was hoarse and I was on my knees begging him for more. Crap.

He moves, bringing a finger to my chin, and lifts it so that my gaze hits his. "You think I'd let someone else touch you?" he asks.

"Uhh..." I'm stumped because once again, I didn't expect him to say that. "I don't know," I mumble.

"No one touches you," he says and bends down to lean close to me. He's a big man, bigger than anyone else I've ever been with. "You're mine. My mate. Do you understand?"

I bite my lip and shake my head. "Not really, we don't have mates or this whole biting them where I'm from." I purse my lips, because that isn't exactly right. "Well, I mean we do but it's more of a spicy move, not a-"

"Not a bite," he growls, and I can tell he doesn't like me calling it that. "It's *our mark*."

"I still don't understand."

He nods and lets out a resigned sigh before he lowers himself onto the bed beside me. "Come here," he says, the command in it unmistakable. Just like before, I move before I think. I grind my teeth together while he settles me into his lap to face him, my legs on either side of his thighs, straddling him.

"You're upset." It's not a question. It's a statement.

"Duh."

"Why?"

"You have to stop making me do what you want, or I'm going to lose my shit."

His hands come to my hips and it's a battle to not think about how big his hands feel on my waist. He makes me feel dainty, almost delicate in a way I've never felt. While I might not be letting myself think about it, my body certainly can't ignore it. I lean forward all too eagerly, letting him bring me closer until I'm flush to his hips. I blush when I realize I can feel the swell of his cock beneath my ass.

"You're strong-willed," he says, leaning back on

the pillows behind him. He looks like a king like this. Completely in repose, relaxed and careless. This man is beautiful. Achingly so. He would make the perfect subject for a renaissance painter, or some ambitious artist conducting a study on the classic form. One summer, I was trying to diversify my courses, which were a little too focused on mathematical theory, so I took an art class. When it came to the human form we had models come in to pose for us. Those were some of the most beautiful people I'd ever seen up close, but the man in front of me has them all beat.

Any painting featuring this man would be perfectly at home on the walls of a fancy ass museum.

But he's not a painting or an art model. He's real, and he's here with me. Wherever here is. I still haven't quite figured out that bit.

I nod. "I've heard that before," I say quietly. Ben said it countless times about me, but in not such straight-forward terms. When he said it, he used words like 'nagging and annoying.' I decide I like being spirited better.

"Spirited," he continues on, fingers starting to play with the end of my braid.

"You make it sound nice," I tell him, looking up

at him. He has a hand at my spine and he's rubbing circles over my lower back. It's soothing.

"There's nothing wrong with a spirited Omega. Only the weak think otherwise."

My brow furrows. "What is that? Omega?"

"It's what you are."

"What those frogs said they made me into, but you still aren't answering my question. I don't know what's going on."

He smiles and drops my braid. "An Omega is the perfect submissive mate. They are for Alphas only." He pauses and his fingertips ghost across the skin of my chin. "No one is worthy of them but the strongest."

My mouth drops open. "*What?*" I whisper. I feel...I feel...I don't know what I feel, but it's not the first time he's called me his mate. "What do you mean *mate*? I-I-I don't understand what you're talking about."

"You're mine. My mate," he says, still lounging. The man is not picking up my panicked as hell vibe, or if he is, he isn't concerned by it. I squeeze my eyes shut and suck in a short breath and run my hands over my face. What the hell am I going to do? I hear a soft purr, it's gentle, barely there, but I know it's to calm me down. He must have just figured out I'm about to have an anxiety attack. "What's wrong?" he asks, and I hear genuine surprise in his voice.

"I don't understand what's going on," I tell him. "This is insane to me. Yesterday I was at a shitty party where my boyfriend cheated on me and then- and then I get snatched by aliens, injected with god knows what, and sold off to the highest bidder. Forgive me if I'm having a hard time keeping up."

He sighs, eyes moving over my face. I see their color clearly now. They aren't fully black like I remember them. They're a soft warm brown with ocher and gold flecks in them. They're beautiful eyes, but of course they are, because everything about this man is beautiful. "I'm sorry," he says, voice gentle in a way that surprises me, "I forget how humans are..."

I bristle at the way he's said 'humans', he definitely said it as if he *wasn't* human. Wait, is he not human? He's big, but...I didn't think there was much difference in us. I raise an eyebrow at him and push away the thought.

"And how are they?"

"Primitive," he replies, as if that explains everything. He looks smug. I want to wipe that look right off his beautiful face. There's something in me that wants to set him on edge. Push him right over a cliff and make him lose the cool look of composure on his face.

I blink at him. "All right, just because we're probably on a spaceship doesn't give you the right to sound so high and mighty. You're wearing leather pants like this is an 80's music video, and you have a wall full of swords," I fling an arm behind me to the sword wall, "some of them look like stuff on the History Channel, and you're calling *humans* primitive?"

He grins and picks up my braid again, tweaking it. "You're funny, too. I like this. I always wanted a clever mate."

Something in me warms at his words.

Clever.

Ben thought I was stuck up sometimes. A know-it-all. But clever? I like that almost as much as I like him calling me spirited. But that doesn't excuse the fact that I have zero idea of what's happening, or that I was *abducted* for pete's sake.

I slap at his hand. "Stop that."

He ignores me and twirls the end of the braid around a finger. "No."

"Swear to god-" A growl comes out of me and I snap my lips shut, eyes wide. Why do I keep making these sounds?

He laughs at the look of surprise on my face and drops my braid then, but only to wrap his arms around me and pull me close. "My mate is fierce. Of course, the All-Mother would give me nothing less."

"What the fuck are you talking about?" I ask, prepared to demand answers on what an All-Mother is, or what this whole 'perfect submissive mate' is about, but my plan goes to shit when he kisses me and I melt like butter in a pan. The fight goes right out of me, and I wrap my arms around him. I lick his bottom lip and he opens his mouth to me, which I take full advantage of. I slant my mouth to his and moan when our tongues meet. I move my tongue along his, taking my time to explore his mouth. His lips are firm but soft against mine, and I like that he lets me take the lead in this kiss. It helps me feel... grounded. Somewhat in control of what's happening. I still don't know where I am, but at least for this moment, this kiss, I'm directing things. I run my hands through his hair and arch my back, pressing my chest against his. He moans and I savor the sound of it, the way it feels against my lips and tongue. My hips roll of their own volition and I grind down on his cock. It's only a second before I feel him start to get hard, the girth of his cock pressing up against my ass. I grind down on him again.

Kissing this man is life altering. I can't even remember what I was mad about. I feel good. Blissed out and hungry for all things *this man*. There's only the kiss and the way our tongues are moving against each other. The way that his hair feels under my hands, or the way I'm rocking against his cock. I move, drop a hand to the sheet bunched around my legs, and shove it to the side. I spread my legs and press myself against him more. I'm starting to get wet, not like before when I couldn't think straight, but my clit is aching now and my hips move faster. When we break apart, I'm breathing hard. I want more.

"Kiss me again," I tell him.

He kisses me again, but this time he's in charge. His hands drop to my ass and he squeezes my flesh hard. I gasp when he starts to direct my rocking and lifts his hips to meet mine. A whine sounds in my throat, but the sound never makes it past my lips, not with him kissing me. He swallows the sound down and moves a hand between us to shove his breeches down and free his cock. I feel it against my thigh, heavy and leaking pre-cum against my skin. I whine again and move forward in a scramble, hips lifting to take him inside of my aching cunt.

The man in front of me, no, not the man, but my

Alpha. My Alpha smells perfectly delicious. I inhale deeply, pulling his scent into my lungs as much as I'm able while kissing him. My hips move at the barest touch of his hands. I follow where he directs, letting him guide me until I'm sinking down on his thick cock. I gasp, but the sound is gone almost as soon as I make it.

"Alpha," I gasp when he lets me go. His hands are on my hips again, fingers digging into my flesh and moving me up and down. I put my hands on his shoulders, bracing myself there for leverage to keep up with the pace he's set. It's fast and my thighs start to burn from the intensity of it, but I'm determined to keep up with him.

His head falls back and he groans, full lips parting as he whispers, "Omega, my sweet little Omega."

There's reverence in the way he says Omega. It's not like when the frogs said it. Leering and greedy. I knew they only wanted me for whatever they could sell me for. That was the only value an Omega had to them, but with my Alpha?

With my Alpha it's as if I'm where his world begins and ends. His hips are moving, snapping up to meet me, the force of it bounces me up and down, right into the rhythm he's dictated. My fingernails dig into his skin where I'm holding onto him, and it's then that I notice the bite.

No, not the bite. *Our mark.*

It's right where mine is. It scars his otherwise perfect skin in a mirror position of where the mark I carry is. It's there, right where his neck meets his shoulder. It's not as big as mine. It's smaller, more delicate in it's position and size, but just as well cared for as the one I carry. It's only another second before I realize it's my work. I orgasm, body going tight from the force of it, and I cry out the only thing I know to scream when I come on this man's cock.

"*Alpha!*"

I pitch forward against his chest, and before I realize what I'm doing, I press my lips to the mark that can only be mine. It's the right shape and size. My mouth pushes to it in a perfect match. I marked him. I bit him. Holy shit. *I bit him back.*

"You are mine." His words are punctuated with the rough rasp of his breath. "Mine. *Mine*," the last word is uttered as a growl against my cheek. He kisses me then and thrusts up into me, roughly bouncing me on his cock. Now that I've come I can tell he's stopped holding back from the rough roll and snap of his hips. His grip on me flexes to the point of pain before I hear him moan his release. I feel the warm release of his cum inside of me. There's so much that it leaks out between us. It's a mess, but I don't care. I move closer to him, wrap my arms tight around his shoulders, and kiss him.

The kiss is as messy as we are, and it's just as good. When we pull apart, he leans his forehead against mine. He looks at me and I can see his beautiful dark eyes scanning my face for a beat before they come back to my eyes.

"My name," he says, "is Ryat."

CHAPTER 6

"I'm Darcy," I whisper.

We stare at each other. We breathe in sync in a way that makes me wonder if he's mimicking what I'm doing. I read somewhere that if you mirror behavior it puts the other person at ease and makes you trust them more. Is that what he's doing with me right now? Is that why I feel like I can trust him, even though I just learned his name? Even though I'm pretty sure he bought me from some frogs?

He smiles. The effect is dazzling. It turns the measure of cruelness I can see in his face and softens it. Makes it endearing and warm. I suspect Ryat isn't a man that gives his smiles freely, but I like that he has no problem sending them my way.

"That is a beautiful name," he says.

I don't know what to say, because until today I've never met anyone named Ryat. Honestly, I didn't even know it was a name, but I want to return the compliment so I say, "Yours is beautiful too."

He huffs out a laugh and I wonder if he knows I've never heard it before. "Darcy," he says again. "DAR-cy...Dar-ceee." He pulls the last syllable long, testing it out I realize, and I smile at him.

"The first one was right," I tell him. "It's just Darcy."

"There's nothing *just* about you."

I suck in a deep breath at his words and I look away quickly. He thinks I'm special. He doesn't have to say it. I can hear it in the way he just said that. The way he speaks to me. I feel tears prick my eyes and I blink them back, trying to put my mind on something else. It's been a very long time since someone spoke to me that way and meant it.

"Thank you," I whisper.

Ryat gathers me close. "You're crying. Why?" He asks. He frowns and nuzzles my neck, lips brushing against the mark on my neck.

"It's nothing."

"Darcy. Do not lie to me." I feel the command in

his voice before I hear it and my mouth opens, the truth spilling out before I can stop it.

"No one has spoken to me like you do in a very long time."

He goes rigid and so do I, but for entirely different reasons.

"Why not?" he asks.

"Because I date assholes," I blurt out, and then grit my teeth. I hadn't meant to answer so quickly but he used *the voice* on me. "Stop using that voice on me," I snap.

"What voice?" He sounds genuinely confused, which just annoys me even more than I already am. "What is an asshole?" he asks. "I will challenge them for you."

I want to laugh at his move to fight assholes for me, but I'm still upset he used *the voice*. I sit back, but don't go far considering he's still inside of me and his hands haven't left my hips. "The one that makes me do what you want."

"Ah, yes, the Alpha command."

I glare at him. He sounds so nonchalant about something that makes me compulsively follow his orders. "Yeah, that. Knock it off."

He frowns at me, eyes moving over my face and then shakes his head. "No."

My mouth drops open and I scuttle back from him. The move forces me to lose his cock and he frowns at me. I turn my face away from him so he doesn't see the look of disappointment that crosses my own face when he slips out of me. God, what I would do to have this man's cock in me 24/7. I don't want to move anymore than he does, but he just said *no to me.*

"What do you mean 'no'?"

Ryat crosses his arms over his broad chest. "Just that. No."

"But why?" I ask and clutch the sheet I had sort of been wearing, but which had definitely come loose during our quickie.

He inclines his head to me like he's telling me a secret. "I know you don't know this as a human," he begins, and I steel myself for whatever it is that Ryat is about to lay on me, "but Omegas do not know what they need."

"Oh they don't?" I snap and pull my legs close to me. I can feel his cum sticky on my thighs and I lift my head higher, not wanting to give away the fact that I'm currently leaking his cum all over the damn sheets while we argue.

"No," he says with a slow shake of his head. "That's why they need Alphas. To show them what they need. Give it to them. It is in an Omega's nature to crave it."

I bristle. "If that's true then why the hell did the frogs have to make me for you?" The question is fair. If what Ryat is saying makes any sense I don't get why there was such a fuss over auctioning off an Omega. The way he makes it sound, Omegas should be looking for Alphas to boss them around. Not the other way around.

He's quiet then. "There was a plague," he says quietly and looks down at his lap, away from me. "It was...severe. We lost," he swallows hard and continues on, "the systems, all of them. Lost almost all of the Omegas. My sisters and mother were among the ones lost."

I swallow hard. "That's terrible. I'm sorry." When I'd asked him why the frogs made me, I never thought he'd say this. I move closer to him until I'm beside him. He looks vulnerable like this, not like the cocky Alpha I was just arguing with, or even the man that might be referred to as 'the Destroyer.'

Right now he simply looks like someone who needs comfort. I want to give him that. "Ryat, I'm sorry," I say again and put a hand on his. My touch is light, mostly because even though we've slept together, even though my fuzzy haze tinged memories tell me it's been days of us doing nothing but having sex, I'm still figuring my way out around him.

He inhales, his chest rising and falling with his breath and he's silent for a second before he looks at me. "There's nothing to be sorry for. The past cannot be changed. All there is, is now." I frown but don't say anything. I grip his hand a little tighter though, and he surprises me when he touches my cheek with his free hand. "You realize I'm not going to let you go home."

It's not a question. It's a statement.

My chest goes tight and I swallow hard. This man is telling me the honest truth. He isn't going to let me go. There's no more home. There's no more Earth. There's no more career that I worked so hard for. But there's also no more feeling like work is the only thing in my life worth noticing. There's no more paying for a house, bills and all of that other bullshit.

There's no more cheating boyfriend who nitpicks me at every turn.

"All there is, is now," I repeat his words quietly and nod that yes, I know, he's not going to be letting me go. He purrs for me. The sound of it warms me up and reminds me that I've never felt more at peace than now. Even through my hazy memories the knowledge that I was cared for, protected, wanted, was a foundation to it all. Waking, I knew it. Even arguing with Ryat now, I know it.

He cups my cheek, fingers tensing slightly along my jaw as he lifts my face so that I look up to meet his gaze. "Your place is with me now."

"I know."

CHAPTER 7

There are two things I know to be true in my short time as an abductee and newly turned Omega This man...this Alpha, is completely devoted to me. And I am never going to see home again. Somehow, one outweighs the other.

I look up from the book in my lap and frown. It's a children's book Ryat got for me. It's supposed to help me with writing, because even though the frogs' helpful implant gave me the ability to understand all two thousand languages of the system, it did not give me the ability to write or read. So here I am reading the equivalent of *Jack and Jill* and trying to learn the alphabet as I go.

There are thirty five letters in the Danarian language. Danarian is pretty, or at least I think it is. It sounds like English to me, but there are some words that are beginning to stick out to me now that I'm trying to read and write.

Eekati means beloved.
Eekati Den is beloved mate.

Ryat says both of these a lot. Especially when he uses his Alpha compulsion on me and I want to kick him in the balls. I don't do that, but I've come close. The Alpha command is something I'm wrestling with, but it's also something he hasn't been abusing.

And of course my favorite, *Drek*. It means fuck.

I say that one a lot, because of course I do. There's a lot of things that deserve the word *drek* directed at them when you're in space.

"What's wrong, *Eekati*?" Ryat comes to stand beside me and runs a hand through my hair. He presses a finger to my furrowed brow when I keep frowning.

"I don't get this. Why is this so hard?"

"It's a complex language," he replies.

"It's been three months...I should be better at this by now." I raise the tablet I'm holding in frustration. It's super lightweight and clear. It looks like it's made entirely out of glass, but it doesn't feel delicate like glass. Whatever it's made out of would have the entire population of tech hungry people back on

Earth going out of their minds to get their hands on it. I'm pretty sure it can handle a lot more than any tablet, computer or phone I've ever owned, but all I've used it for so far is slowly reading children's books.

"Be patient," Ryat advises, but I keep frowning. I'm used to excelling at academic centered things. Not getting the language pisses me off, but at least I'm not alone in it. I look over at the other women here with me. All of the women Ryat rescued with me are sitting with tablets like mine. They are all studying up on the language too, though some with more success than me. Rose is beaming as she pages through her tablet. No doubt reading the equivalent of *War and Peace* in Danarian at the rate she's been learning.

Sally sighs in frustration. "She's right. This blows." There's a murmur of agreement from the others, but then Nill is breezing in with a tray of food.

Turns out Rose was right about him, he was all right. He didn't like the slave trading his people were doing, and he decided to do something about it. He left with us when Ryat bought all of us. Apparently the Magi, which are the species Nill is, were pissed at losing all of us, even to a Royal Alpha. It was a big embarrassment for the auction to get crashed in front of so many spectators—which I learned was composed of some of the highest rollers in this solar system. The Magi, Nill informed me, are pretty vain as a whole, and the second Ryat had us out of the auction room they decided they weren't going to take the embarrassment lying down.

"There was a plan to attack," he explained when I joined the rest of the women. "I thwarted it by rerouting the missiles."

"Reroute them where?" I asked.

"The Magi ship."

Yup. Nill blew the ship right out of the...sky? *Space?* Whichever way you looked at it, he blew up the ship and hopped a ride with us. Or rather, he was floating in an escape pod and Rose brought him aboard.

I was right about her just like she was right about Nill. Rose is a smart cookie and watched far more than the Magi realized during her time as their prisoner. She's a whiz with alien tech and has, on more than one occasion, piloted the ship we're on.

"The Royal Alpha is right. Danarian is one of the more complex languages in the system. It will take time to achieve even moderate fluency. It took me years of study."

He sets the tray down beside Rose and I bite back a smile when I see her pluck a treat off the tray and thank Nill. He always makes sure she eats first. It's hard to find Rose without Nill nearby. I think the two of them have a thing for one another.

Sally shoves her tablet to the side and gets up to snag a snack from the tray. "How much longer till we're on Danar?" she asks.

We've been enroute for weeks now. We didn't immediately head there, not with what happened at the auction. Ryat said there were too many people looking for us. Too many Alphas wanting an Omega of their own. Ones who would want to test me to see if I was really an Omega. How they would do that, I don't know. But I do know Omegas are rare, and they are desperately sought after.

I didn't get it at first, but now I do.

Only Alphas can reproduce with Omegas. Only Omegas are born to Alpha and Omega pairings, but the plague wiped them all out. It's a big messed up situation for the species that rely on Omegas to reproduce, of which I learned there are dozens and dozens.

The Danarians are just one of them. With the plague his people were on the brink of dying out, but now there's hope. Nill knows how the Magi created me, and how they planned to make more Omegas. With a little luck, and the resources on Danar, there might be a way to recreate that with the women on the ship. Surprisingly, none of them want to go back home. Turns out their life, like mine, wasn't that great either.

Ryat reaches down and squeezes my hand as if sensing my thoughts, which he probably does given the bond between us. It's helpful in a lot of situations, but I'm still getting used to him poking around in my head for my mood when I'm angry at him. Right now, it's okay though.

"Another day or so," he tells them. "I've sent word ahead about our arrival so that preparations can be made."

I watch all the women tense in the room. Reality is setting in, I think. At least it is for me. So far we've been sequestered on this ship in our own little bubble. It's weird and alien, especially when you look outside of a window and *see the inky blackness of space*. Or just push a button on one little machine to have food appear instantly, but it's become familiar. That's all coming to an end, and I know what's going through their minds. They're worried we'll be separated when we land.

"Everything will be taken care of," Ryat tells them, sensing the mood shift.

I clear my throat and put my tablet down. I have to be the one to calm them down, afterall, I'm going to be a queen. Yes, a queen. Not *the* Queen, because I don't think Danar operates like that, but a queen is still a queen. And there's no time like the present to start acting...queenly?

"Ah, what will happen when we arrive? Will we be able to stay together?" I ask. The women lean forward watching and listening.

Ryat's lips purse. "Is that...what you want?" he asks me, but I know the question is for the entire group. Even Nill is listening in with as much focus as the rest of us.

"Yes, it's what we want. We want to stay together, and," I pause, because I know there's more, "if they turn into Omegas, I want them to choose their mates."

Ryat pauses then. I know that one is a tough sell. I didn't get to choose him, but it still feels right to me. Besides, I'd pick Ryat over being sold to any one of those faces on the tech screens any day of the week.

"Bonding and mating are delicate circumstances, but I will ensure Omegas are pleased with their mates."

There's a collective *whoosh* as the breath the women had been holding is let out. "And of course, you may stay together if you wish. I'll have accommodations made."

"And what about Nill?" I ask. I can't forget him. He's the reason why we weren't blown out of the sky. Everyone tenses again for the answer, because Nill has become a beloved part of our group. I don't know if word has gotten out about what he did to save us, and the last thing I want is him looking over his shoulder on Danar for anyone wanting revenge.

"He'll be safe. I'm appointing him to the head of a research team. There will be security and privileges with that position," Ryat answers smoothly, and I relax. Of course he has a plan without even skipping a beat. My Alpha always has a plan.

Always.

He considers the room for a second and then asks, "Is this all agreeable?"

The women nod and a chorus of yes's is heard. They're happy. Good. If they're happy, then so am I.

I smile when I feel Ryat's hand in my hair. I don't even have to look at him to know he's smiling too. Because if I'm happy, then he is too. I rise to my feet and hug my Alpha, bury my nose into the crook of his neck. My lips graze across *our mark.*

The mark I gave him. I feel his fingers brush over the one I carry as well.

Our match was not by choice. It's not the future I thought I would have for myself, but all of this, the alien abduction, me almost getting sold off and then mated to an Alpha I didn't know. I wouldn't change it.

This is our future, and I would choose it again and again if I had to.

THANK YOU! <3

I didn't think I'd ever be brave enough to write this little book, or plan not one but two series! I have to thank Booktok and the big wide world of amazingly supportive romance readers! Creating this world, these characters, all the fun love stories...all of it has been a badass journey for yours truly.

Darcy and Ryat were characters I had in my head for a good long while. I could see them plain as day and wanted to give them a go at an HEA. Ryan and Darcy's love story will become a known legend in my Omegaverse world and you bet your cute, flawless, booty this won't be the last you hear or see of them.

I hope you loved *Royally Claimed!* This is the first installment in my *Royally Claimed series.* I wanted to take my time and introduce you all to my weird amazing little ABO universe. In case you're new here and didn't know ABO = Alpha, Beta, Omega dynamics. This is the foundation I built my Spicy Space Omegaverse on. I love to write growly Alphas and their perfectly ornery Omega counterparts. *The Royally Claimed Series* is my first publishing foray into this amazingly satisfying world and I cross my fingers you stick with me on it!

My Brutal Alpha is on the way and you can expect exclusive content drops for my newsletter bbys.

Sign up here and don't miss a thing!
https://bit.ly/Jupiternews

MY BRUTAL ALPHA TEASER
PROLOGUE

You know those paintings in all the hotel lobbies or doctor's offices that have landscapes? The big paintings in libraries that have a seaside town with a path leading off into the distance? Or the boring photos that have a car or boat barely visible on the horizon? The ones really just meant to occupy some wall space in a place no one really wants to be?

Well, when I was a kid I used to *love* those. It wasn't for the artistic talent or anything like that. I mean, these pictures, paintings, collages, mosaics—whatever the medium, were never meant to inspire. No, it wasn't the art value of it, or the aesthetics of the crappy landscape in a too shiny gold frame that called to me. It was because I wanted to be on that ship at sea, in one of those small houses on the cliff, or walking on that path to nowhere.

If I concentrated as hard as I could, I could narrow my world down until the idea of that house perched high above the ocean, the smoke rising merrily from it's chimney, seemed almost real. The boat someone hastily painted to create the illusion of distance and depth taking me to some far away destination where I could start again—where I would be new. Those paths to nowhere told me I could keep walking and walking, *and just walking*, until the life I was in was so far behind me that when I thought about it, it would seem like nothing more than a bad dream.

I'd get caught daydreaming on the regular as a kid, staring off at the mediocre landscape that had become, for all purposes, my escape. My ma calling my name over and over until she finally reached over and grabbed me, giving me a hard shake and bringing my ass right back to reality.

I guess it's easy to figure out my life as a kid sucked. I mean, it really did suck. It was the worst.

I worked hard to leave that behind, moved away from home for college and studied hard. But then my dad got cancer and I had to move back to take care of him. He'd gotten better, which should have been a cause for celebration. It was just a celebration that I had always thought would include me. My ma hadn't even stuck around when the treatments had been the worst, but he'd had other ideas. He moved right on without me in the pursuit of making the most of his life.

Making the most of his life meant he remarried and now has two new kids in a big new house, and frequent trips to Europe. What it didn't mean was helping his *"drop out kid"* sort out finances to go back to college. Even though I'd dropped everything my sophomore year for him. I'd been out of school for five years and I felt lost as hell in getting back into the rhythm of it. I had zero idea what I wanted to do with my life, had worked as a sales clerk for minimum wage in a dress shop I couldn't afford to actually buy anything in, and was pretty much an orphan.

Yes, I know, my adult life also sucks.

Which brings me to my next point of concern. My abduction. Yes, abduction. For all my wishing as a kid, wanting to vanish into a painting, be on a journey to nowhere, my ever-elusive path *away* from my life, the thing I never thought would happen —*happened.*

I got away from my life. I did it in a big way, all

right. Which isn't necessarily a terrible thing, because remember the part where I said my life was shit? *College dropout, minimum wage job, no parents or real home?*

Getting away from that was, well...getting away from that is everything I ever wanted. But the way it happened could have happened a lot better. But of course, it went the way it did, because it was me. Things never went to plan when it *was me*.

It could have happened with me winning the lotto, or landing a fancy new job. Hell, even me getting back into my state college would have been a-okay with me. But none of those things happened. The way I got my new start, my brand new adventure that I had spent my entire life wishing for, was that I got abducted by an alien.

At least, I think he's an alien?

Either way, I don't understand him, and he doesn't understand me.

And none of this can be good, because *it's me.*

CHAPTER 1

"Are you going out tonight?"

I look up from the dress display I've been fiddling with for the better part of an hour to see my coworker Janice. "What?"

"Are you going out tonight?" she asks, slower this time, like she's talking to a child. I roll my eyes.

"No," I say with a quick shake of my head.

"Oh, come on! You never go out, Tally."

"It's because I'm broke, Janice."

I go back to my work, fully intending to ignore Janice and her perfectly reasonable question for a Friday night. It's just before closing and we're young and alive and in the prime of our life, or whatever it is that spurs people my age to go out and enjoy themselves. I'm not one of those people. Mostly because what I said to Janice is true. I am broke as shit. I have enough to cover rent and the couple of small loans I'd taken out to go to school, plus my car, but after that? I had just about enough left to buy myself a cheap bottle of wine from the Trader Joe's down the street and maybe spring for a knock off pizza.

Pizza, below average wine and whatever I could stream that night, was my definition of a wild Friday night. It wasn't the same for Janice. She worked here because she liked the clothes, which were all pretty and trendy, a little more upscale than your usual stuff, but all way out of my price range–even with the store discount.

I ignore Janice even though she's letting out a sigh that sounds like it's pulled from every suffering Victorian lady that ever existed. I fold the tops, fluff the scarves, and then move on to the jewelry. I want to get this display done so we can lock up and I can get on my merry way to a two dollar bottle of wine. Janice isn't helping us get closer to clocking off, even though she's supposed to be sweeping. I'll probably have to do that when I'm done here, which is fine if I could just decide on a set up. It just looks cluttered, but I bet if I moved the necklaces to the side and-

"What if I paid your way?" she asks, and I can't ignore that.

"What?" I ask, all thoughts of necklaces and sweeping gone right out the window, because it's a Friday night and I can count the number of times I'd actually let myself cut loose. Just because I couldn't afford to have fun didn't mean I didn't want to.

"I'll pay for everything tonight if you just come out," Janice says, hands going to her hips. "And I mean *everything*. Drinks, food, cover charge," she waves a hand at the store around me, "pick out a dress even, because…" She tilts her head to the side, eyes moving over me before she says, "what you have on isn't really the vibe for tonight, Tally."

I wrinkle my nose and look down at what I'm wearing. "What I'm wearing is fine," I gripe, even though I know she's right. I look like a librarian in sensible slacks, loafers and a blue button up. I'm surprised I'm not given more grief for how I dress, with the clothes we're meant to be selling, but I guess most people don't pay that much attention to the shop girl. Janice, by comparison, is the very definition of the "cool girl." Stylish in an effortless way that I love so much on her, because the woman knows how to dress herself. She's pretty too, which only adds to her allure. Today she's wearing a baby blue sheath dress, pink chunky heels that should not work, but do, and an assortment of rings and necklaces.

"Yeah, uh-huh," Janice mutters, turning towards the racks at her back. There's nothing but sparkly party dresses there, and jewel-tone high slit gowns that I've looked at several times a day since we got them last week. I'd never be able to afford one, seeing as it's almost a third of my rent, but it's nice to dream.

I really liked to dream. When you dreamed there was nothing but possibility, and the promise of something better. When you dreamed, you got to leave behind reality, even if only for a little while. Those dresses were part of my dream, which is why I didn't move or understand what the hell Janice was up to right away when she snags one and waves it at me.

"Put this on. I'll find shoes," she orders, tossing the dress at me on her way past to the back of the store. The dress, a deep lush red, hits me square in the chest and I barely catch it before it hits the ground.

"What? You can't buy me this!"

"Sure, I can. You know my dad is loaded. It's fine."

"Janice, no!"

"I have the AMEX card, I'm buying it. Now, do you think the gold, or silver?" she asks, holding up a pair of strappy heels. I debated telling her neither and giving her back the dress to slink off to my perfectly safe and predictable Friday night, because I wasn't raised to take money like this. Especially when someone's dad was unknowingly footing the bill—but all I can think of is that I'll get to live out my dream. I'll put the dress on, the shoes, the whole thing, and have a night to party.

"The gold," I say, and she nods in agreement.

"Thought so too. Get changed now. I'll ring this up and we're out of here, baby!"

I hesitate, because this sounds way too good to be true. I like Janice, I like her a whole lot, but we've never really spent a ton of time together. We work together often and have gotten coffee a time or two, but this...her buying me an entire outfit that I know isn't cheap, and offering to cover the whole night? That's a lot.

"Are you sure?" I ask.

Janice looks up from the register where she's already brandishing her dad's shiny card. "Get changed or so help me god, Tally. We have a club to get to!"

That gets my feet moving.

A club.

I've never been to a club in my entire life.

I hustle towards the dressing room, nearly tripping over the skirt of the flowing dress in my excitement, but I manage to get it together and change in record time. I'm barely exiting the dressing room when Janice shoves the newly purchased heels into my hands and demands I turn around with a wave.

"Let me get the tag off. Get those on, and let's get the hell out of here."

'What do I do with my clothes, though?" I ask. The bundle of clothes I'd worn to work that day sit on top of my backpack.

She wrinkles her nose at the sight. "A backpack, Tally? Really?"

"What? It holds everything I need," I protest, and Janice rolls her eyes.

"We're stashing that under the register. You work tomorrow anyways, right? You can get it then."

I nod, wincing at the thought of waking up bright and early to catch the half hour bus from my small cramped apartment into work the next day. "Yeah, I'm in at eight."

Janice makes a face. "Like, in the morning? The AM time?" she asks, not bothering to hide her disgust. I know Janice is well off. I think she told me one time her dad was a hedge fund investor or something. I don't know. Whatever it is, it's enough to get shiny black AMEX cards and daughters who refuse to do anything before noon.

"Yeah, that's the one."

"Gross. Why are you in so early?" she asks, yanking the tag off the dress. She snags my backpack, shoves my clothes inside, and makes for the register.

"It's inventory," I say, sitting and putting on the heels.

"So?"

"I need the hours," I say, but don't go into it. Janice knows I work a lot, but I've never said why. I'm grateful she doesn't pry. I don't want to think too much about the why right now. Not when I'm so close to having the kind of night I've daydreamed about while putting away fancy dresses not meant for me.

Janice makes a sound that tells me she doesn't get it. "I mean, I guess..."

"Hey, where is this club again? Is there gonna be food, because I haven't eaten since breakfast and I'm about to be hangry," I say, the whole direction of our conversation starting to make me uncomfortable. I don't hide that I have to save a lot more, and that things are tight, not from Janice, who is as close to a friend as anyone the past few years.

My heart pangs. It's painful, the ache I feel at

remembering the friends I had before. At college. Lots of them. My roommate and I had been amazing friends before I'd vanished. I'd even been a part of a few extracurricular clubs. I was a regular with intramurals, tennis, and I had almost pledged to the new sorority that had come to campus the semester I'd withdrawn. I'd been social and friendly, but now all I did was work and count the dollars in my bank account—the account that never seemed to go up.

I didn't go out. I didn't make friends. Janice was close as it got, and this was our first actual night out on the town. I'd known her for two years. Jesus. I didn't like thinking about that.

It was sad. I knew that. It was no way to live, but I just kept going, telling myself it would change next month, next year. Maybe I'd catch a windfall somewhere and things would turn around, but things just kept on as they were with nothing changing. Just the same routine day-after-day with no end in sight.

Tonight could be a break in all of that, though.

This was different, and I didn't care how early I had to wake up, or if my bus broke down again making me have to switch, or the fact that when the sun rose I'd be back in my sensible boring clothing and toting my overstuffed backpack around again.

I had tonight to be whoever I wanted. And the

woman that I wanted to be wore fancy dresses and went to clubs. She'd drink too much and laugh too loud. She had friends.

"I mean, I think so, but we can get something on the way over, okay?" Janice asks. She gives my bag one last shove and then holds up a purse from the display beside her. "I bought you this too. Shove your phone in and let's go, okay? I already called the car, and it's outside."

Tonight the woman I was choosing to be was the kind that had friends.

Read on in *My Brutal Alpha!*

My life wasn't great. I worked too much, and I had zero fun. All I wanted to do was escape and start over. One night the universe decided to grant me my wish. It should have been a good thing, right?

Wrong.

My brand new adventure, one that I spent my entire life wishing for, happened because I got

abducted by an alien. I mean, the alien is really, really hot and sexy, ***but still.*** And that's not even touching on the fact that he keeps calling me his mate.

Pre-Order **My Brutal Alpha**

My Brutal Alpha is a full-length novel and can be read on its own, apart from the prequel novella Royally Claimed. You don't need to read both to understand the plot, but the world building will be richer if you start at the beginning!

Sign up for my newsletter https://bit.ly/Jupiternews to get the latest on My Brutal Alpha's release. I'll be doing a cover reveal and chapter teases there, bby!

ABOUT THE AUTHOR

Jupiter Belle is a brand spankin' new spicy space romance author just trying to figure it all out. Currently, she's got one series on deck and another in the works. If you love ABO dynamics, Omegaverse crack fics and spicy everything, then be this wildling's friend!

Sign up for my newsletter https://bit.ly/Jupiternews